AR

Folk Tales from Chile

Brenda Hughes

illustrated by
Dick de Wilde

Hippocrene Books, Inc.
New York

Hippocrene Books, Inc. edition, 1999.

Originally published in 1962 by George G. Harrap & Co. Ltd., London.

For information, address:
HIPPOCRENE BOOKS, INC.
171 Madison Avenue
New York, NY 10016

Library of Congress Cataloging-in-Publication Data:
Hughes, Brenda.
Folk tales from Chile / Brenda Hughes ; illustrated by Dick de Wilde.
p. cm.
Summary: An illustrated collection of fifteen traditional Chilean tales that "represent a fusion . . . of the Old World culture of the Spanish soldier and priest and the native Indian culture of ancient Chile."
ISBN 0-7818-0712-3
1. Tales—Chile [1. Folklore—Chile.] I. De Wilde, Dick, ill. II. Title.
PZ8.1.H873713Fo 1998
[398.2'0983]—dc21 98-36881
CIP
AC

Printed in the United States of America

Preface

THE FIRST invaders of Chile were the Peruvians from the north, who, in the fifteenth century, advanced to a certain point and made all that part of Chile a vassal of the Empire of the Incas. When the Spaniards, under their commander, Francisco Pizarro, conquered Peru some troops continued into Chile. Pizarro granted rights over that country to his favorite subordinate, Pedro de Valdivia, the founder of the modern capital of Santiago.

The original inhabitants of Chile were Indians belonging to various tribes, of whom the most independent were the Araucanians of the forests of southern Chile. They were never truly defeated and clung tenaciously to their own language, customs, and beliefs. The Spaniards imposed their language, rule of law, and Catholicism upon the rest of Chile.

These folk-tales therefore represent a fusion of two basic strains—the Old World culture of the Spanish soldiers and priests and the native Indian culture of ancient Chile. Some of the stories persist in folk-songs and recitations to the present day. Others were recorded by diligent Spanish priests who accompanied the conquistadores. Many of the superstitions and beliefs were told to European scholars and travellers who journeyed through the region from the nineteenth century onward. Chilean, English, United States, German, and French sources have been consulted. It is believed that this is the first children's collection of Chilean folk-tales to be made outside Chile.

B.H.

Contents

The White Cloud's Daughter

THERE WAS once a spirit who lived in the heart of a volcano. This spirit fell in love with a pretty white cloud and took her away with him to the top of his mountain. He was extremely possessive and did not want anyone else to see how pretty she was.

"Now that you are my wife," he told her, "you must stay shut up in my mountain."

"But I like being in the open air," pleaded the white cloud. "I like looking down on the earth and seeing everything that goes on."

But her pleas were in vain. The spirit kept her imprisoned. Not long afterwards a daughter was born to her, and looked just like her mother. The spirit was delighted, and called the child Snow-white, because she was the whitest creature he had ever seen. Now that the white cloud had her daughter to care for she did not fret so much, but she did not forget the world outside.

One day, finding the spirit had left the entrance to

the mountain open, the white cloud went out, holding her baby in her arms. Just at that moment she caught sight of the wind, who was the spirit's worst enemy. Afraid, she tried to run back to safety in the depths of the mountain, but it was too late. The wind swept her up in his arms, and in her desperate struggle she dropped her baby daughter.

The spirit of the mountain returned just as his wife was being carried away by the wind. He fumed and raged, but could not rescue the white cloud. His anger was so fierce that the earth trembled as he shouted, and the fire in the heart of the mountain gushed forth. Streams of molten lava began to pour down from the top of the mountain. Smoke curled in menacing patterns against the sky, and the Indians living in the villages at the foot of the mountain hurriedly snatched up their belongings and took shelter by the sea until the spirit's anger ceased.

Now the spirit had a faithful servant who used to accompany him on his travels. He was a kind-hearted dwarf.

"Whenever I am away you must stay inside the mountain and look after Snow-white," ordered the spirit. "Be sure you never let her go out of the mountain at any time, night or day. If you guard her well, when she is grown up you shall have her for your wife."

This pleased the dwarf well, and he cared for the girl so devotedly that she became very fond of him.

Year after year went by, and she saw only her father, the spirit, and the kind dwarf, her friend. Sometimes her mother, the white cloud, would come to the mountain, carried by the wind, hoping to see her daughter. But it was no use. Snow-white was too well guarded by the kind dwarf. The white cloud would weep with disappointment, and her tears would roll down the mountain-side, carving swift torrents, which overflowed their banks, flooding the Indian villages at the foot of the mountain.

If ever the spirit returned in time to catch sight of the white cloud hovering over the top of the mountain he fumed and raged, so that fire came out of the volcano, and all the time the white cloud wept and the rivers rose higher and higher.

Snow-white grew so lovely that the kind dwarf could not refuse her any request. She pleaded with him to let her go outside the mountain, and finally he agreed, on condition that she went out at night when she could not be seen, and that she always returned before dawn to the heart of the mountain. These were the hours she loved best, when she could feel the cool air on her face and lift her eyes to the bright stars.

One night she said to the dwarf, "Fetch me down a star so that I can wear it on my forehead!"

The dwarf sighed.

"I am not tall enough to reach the sky," he said sadly. "Only your father, the spirit, can do that."

"Very well, tell him to get it for me," ordered the girl.

But the dwarf was unwilling to do that, for then the spirit would know that he had been disobeyed. However, the girl said she would never marry the dwarf unless he did what she asked, so he went away to find the spirit. In his haste he forgot to shut the entrance to the mountain.

Next morning Snow-white saw a gleam of light and discovered she could push open the rock door and make her own way out into the world. She had never been outside in the daytime before. For the first time in her life she could see the sunshine, the flowers, the birds, and she was enchanted by the beauty all around her. She climbed all round the mountain, forgetting to be tired because the world was so wonderful. But by the time she reached the mountain-top she was ready to fall asleep, and lay down on a flat rock.

Her mother, the white cloud, floating by, tried to draw a cover over her sleeping daughter, for she knew it was dangerous for the girl to stay there, but the wind carried the white cloud away before she could do anything to protect Snow-white.

Then the sun blazed forth, and, catching sight of the lovely girl asleep on the mountain-top, bent down in order to kiss her. At the touch of his kiss the girl, already tired out, simply melted away. And when the spirit and the kind dwarf came to look for the girl, all they found was a clear spring of cool water where she had been sleeping. Their beautiful Snow-white had left them forever.

The Pincoya's Daughter

THERE WAS once a very poor Indian woman who lived in a little hut by the seashore. She was so old that all her relations and friends had died long ago, but she went on living by herself and managed to eat and to keep warm. She was no longer strong enough to work in the fields, like the other villagers, so she spent most of her time on the beach where she collected sea food and birds' eggs.

Sometimes great storms would spring up and the old woman did not dare stir out of her tumbledown hut. As soon as the winds were calm, however, she would hurry out, for those were the times when the little pools amid the rocks would be full of shrimps and tiny crabs and baby fish of all kinds. Piles of driftwood, too, from some unhappy shipwreck would be driven up the beach by the strong breakers, and then the old woman felt very pleased with life, for it meant she had plenty of firewood just for the taking.

On the morning after the very worst storm the old

woman could remember she went out as usual along the beach and found a fine big crab.

"The biggest crab I have seen for years," she murmured happily to herself. "Well, at least I shan't be hungry to-day!"

She placed the crab carefully in her basket, on top of some other smaller fish, and went home. But by the time she reached her hut and unpacked the basket on her table she was upset to discover that the crab had split into two halves.

"Oh, dear, and I was so careful with it," lamented the old woman. "I must have broken it when I put it in the basket."

She took a sharp cooking-knife to open the shell in order to scoop out the meat, but, to her amazement, inside the crab was nothing but a beautiful living child. From the waist upward she looked like a red-haired Indian girl, with a fair complexion, but below the baby had a shiny fish's tail.

"What ever am I to do with you?" asked the old woman. "You are so beautiful I should like to keep you, but I don't know how to look after you."

She covered the baby up again in the crab shell and, carrying it very carefully, visited the wise woman of the village, who listened silently to her story and examined the baby girl for a long time. At last the wise woman spoke.

"She is not the daughter of any human parents, that I can tell you. I am sure she is the child of one of the sea fairies, the pincoyas. Perhaps her mother put her in the crab shell for safety during the bad storm, to save her from being eaten by the hungry sea wolves who prowl on the ocean floor."

"But what am I to do with her?" asked the old woman. "Suppose I do her harm, without meaning to, but just because I don't know how to treat baby pincoyas?"

"Take her back to the seashore," advised the wise woman. "Sit her on a rock where she may be seen, but safely out of danger from the waves. Keep yourself out of sight, and watch to see what happens."

So the baby pincoya, sleeping peacefully in her shell, was taken back to the beach. The old woman lodged her securely on a warm, dry rock and hid herself near by. Presently she heard a woman singing in a strange language, and from the seventh wave a glittering, red-haired creature emerged. Her body gleamed like mother of pearl when the red glow of sunset colors it, and her eyes were as changeable as the sea when the wind ruffles its surface.

The pincoya saw her child, and went up to her, afraid she might have come to some harm. When she was sure her daughter was quite unhurt, she picked the baby up, and crooned a lullaby, like any human mother. She did not look at all frightening or magical, so the old Indian woman found the courage to leave her hiding-place. She told the pincoya how she had found the crab shell, and taken it home, thinking it was just an ordinary crab.

"You have saved my child's life," said the pincoya. "I was afraid the sea wolves would take her away from me, and she cannot swim by herself yet, so I hid her for safety in the shell, but the great storm swept her to land."

The Indian woman promised to help the pincoya in any way she could.

"Take my child home with you, and look after her for a little while longer," asked the pincoya. "She will be safe with you. I will see that every morning all the rock pools are full to the brim with fish and shrimps and everything you like most. You shall never be hungry again."

This was one of the special powers of the pincoya, as the Indian woman well knew, so she agreed at once. The child made her home in the old woman's hut, but every day she was taken to the beach, where her mother could come out of the sea to feed her and play with her. So the months went by, so quickly that the old woman hardly noticed them. She never went short of food, and the growing little pincoya was the joy of her life.

"If only things could stay like this for ever," said the Indian to herself.

But every day the child grew stronger, and her foster-mother knew that only too soon would come the time when the baby pincoya would be big enough to swim fearlessly in the ocean. The Indian went to the wise woman for advice.

"I may not live much longer, for I am old," she said. "But I would like to keep the little pincoya as long as I can. If I kept her with me at home her mother would be powerless to take her away."

The wise woman shook her head.

"The pincoya would know all about it," she said, "and when you went along the shore there would be no more shrimps for you to collect, no more fine-tasting crabs. Besides, if the people of the village knew, they would drive you away, and the little pincoya too."

The old woman sighed. In her heart she had known all along there was no help for it. Humans and creatures of the sea could not live together for ever. She gave the wise woman a gift of fish and went home.

At last the time came when the pincoya began to teach her child to swim, starting in the sheltered deep pools near the beach, then gradually venturing farther and farther out to sea. One morning the pincoya told the old woman that she was ready to claim her daughter.

Tears ran down the old woman's cheeks.

"She is still too small, too young," she pleaded. "Let her stay with me a few more days."

"Do not grieve so," said the pincoya. "We must obey the laws of the sea world, but we will never forget you, and we promise to return to you often."

So the old woman was left alone once more, but things were not quite as they had been before. No matter what the weather, the shore near her hut was always teeming with tiny fish, so that she could always fill her basket and never went hungry. And every so often the baby pincoya, who all too quickly grew as tall and handsome as her mother, would leap out of the water and greet her foster-mother with much affection, bringing her each time a lustrous pearl from the sea-bed as a token of her love. In this way the old woman lived quietly and happily until she died.

The Magic Cow

MANY YEARS ago there lived a boy called Sancho and his baby sister, Maria. Their father, Joaquin, worked hard on their tiny farm, helped by their mother, Dolores, and although they were not rich they were not poor either. Soon Maria would be one year old, and her parents planned to make it a day to remember.

"I shall sell the russet cow at the market," Joaquin decided, "and the money she brings will pay for presents for every one."

Sancho heard these words and ran up to his father. For as long as he could remember, and he was now twelve years old, the russet cow had been his closest friend. He often talked to her as if she were another human being, and she would look back at him so intelligently that he was convinced she understood every word he said.

"Please, father, say you will not sell our cow—say you will never sell her!" he pleaded breathlessly.

"But one day I shall sell her," his father said, not realizing how much Sancho loved the russet cow. "This is as good a time as any. Don't you want Maria to have a fine birthday?"

Sancho said no more but went outside to say good-bye to his friend. She gave him a long, sad stare, as if she knew very well what was going to happen to her, and she mooed softly four times in farewell. Next morning, very early, before the children were awake, Joaquin set off for market, leading the russet cow.

The market where the most buyers were to be found was in a village on the other side of the river, so Joaquin rode along the bank until he came to a ford. Before he could settle his horse to cross he was stopped by a strange woman who suddenly appeared in the path from behind a bush.

"I must cross the river," she cried. "Be kind to a poor woman, good sir, and let her sit behind you on your fine horse, while you ride across."

She looked quite harmless, so Joaquin nodded his head and helped her climb up behind him. He did not know that she was a witch, a kalku, hated and feared by the Indians of that part.

All went well until Joaquin was in mid-stream, when suddenly the kalku muttered some strange words, and the horse, with Joaquin and the kalku on its back, was sucked down into a great hole in the bed of the river. This hole led to an underground road, along which the horse began to gallop at a frightening pace, so that within seconds the three of them had disappeared.

The russet cow had been several steps behind, and when the hole opened up in front of the horse she managed to turn to one side and avoid being pulled down into the depths. She tossed her head in sorrow at losing her master, then turned round, climbed up the river-bank, and wandered peacefully home by herself to the farm. Sancho was overjoyed to see his old friend, but Dolores could not understand what had happened, and became more and more anxious about her husband. No word came from him that night, nor the next, nor any time at all, and as month after month went by Dolores was forced to agree with her neighbours that her husband would never come back.

"If your father has gone for good," Dolores said to the children, "we shall have to sell the farm and move to the village where I was born."

"Must we sell the russet cow too?" asked Sancho anxiously.

His mother shook her head. She did not want to take away Sancho's dearest friend.

They moved to a tiny house with some land quite close to the sea. Very little would grow on the stony fields, and in any case there was no man to work the land. Without the faithful cow to give plenty of milk the family would have been hungry indeed. Maria grew strong and happy, toddling after her brother along the seashore, following him round the fields. Sancho took great care of his little sister, and when he was busy fishing he would see that she was perched safely on some rocks clear of the waves.

One day, when Sancho had been lucky with his catch, and the sun shone warmly, the children decided to bathe. Sancho was a fine swimmer, but all that Maria could do was to sit in the shallow water and splash happily. Suddenly the sky darkened, and a great wave hurtled towards them. Sancho was caught up, flung head over heels, flung against the sand, and knocked down again and again each time he tried to stand upright. At last the waves died down and he could keep his balance, but he soon became frightened when he realized that Maria was nowhere to be seen.

He dived under the waves, opening his eyes to peer

at the sea bottom, but he did not see his sister. She had vanished utterly.

Too tired to swim any more, afraid of what his mother would say, Sancho sat on the beach, the tears rolling down his cheeks. If only there were something he could do!

"Sancho, Sancho, stop crying and listen to me," whispered a gentle voice in his ear.

The boy glanced up and was astonished to see the russet cow. At first he could not believe she was actually talking to him, but when she opened her mouth again he knew it must be true.

"The same witch who stole your father and his horse has taken Maria away," the cow went on. "She is a sea witch and very clever. Unless you listen very carefully to what I say, it will be your turn next."

"Is my father really alive, then? And Maria? Can I save them? Please tell me what to do!" exclaimed Sancho breathlessly.

"First you must kill me," said the cow very calmly. "Then you must skin me and throw the skin on the sea. It will float and turn into a boat. Climb into the boat and be sure to hold fast to my tail. If you are in any danger, pull a hair out from my tail and it will save you."

Sancho stared in dismay at the cow.

"But I cannot kill you, my friend," he said. "You are my very best friend; I could never hurt you."

"You must," repeated the cow, "and you must do

it quickly. There is no time to lose. But remember, after you have killed me cut out my cyes and put them in your pocket. They are magic eyes, and will help you to see any place you wish, even if it is under the sea or inside a mountain or miles over the horizon."

So Sancho took out his big clasp-knife and killed the russet cow. Then he skinned the animal, and cut out the eyes. The skin was thrown on to the water, where it became a light, round boat, dancing on the water as if eager to drift out to sea.

Sancho swam after it, and as he did so he noticed some large, fierce fish biting at the cow's feet, trying to pull the boat away with them to the bottom of the sea. The boy caught up with the boat and pulled out a hair from the tail. At once the hair turned into a big stick, with which he hit the fish until they let go. The last fish to do so was the biggest of them all, and the stick broke in half on its back. But the fish made off, which was all that Sancho cared about, and he climbed safely into the boat.

Night was now falling, and Sancho took one of the cow's eyes and held it to his eye like a telescope. Through it he could see right down to the ocean bed. Everything looked calm and peaceful, so he put the eye safely back in his pocket and slept, while the boat drifted all night long at the mercy of the wind and currents.

The warm sun of morning awakened him, and he sat up at once, alert to danger. As he watched, the blue sky was blotted out by the wings of many birds, black as night and bigger than condors, which swooped down and alighted upon the boat. Their weight forced the boat lower and lower into the water, until it was about to submerge.

Quickly Sancho pulled out another hair from the cow's tail, and this time it changed into a rifle. He took aim and fired, and one by one the birds dropped into the sea, staining it a dull red.

"Bless you, my friend," he said cheerfully, patting the side of the boat as if it were still the flank of the russet cow.

On they drifted southward, and soon Sancho saw icebergs glittering in the sun. He looked through the cow's eye and saw a pretty little island on which was built a fine castle, encircled by high walls. Sancho felt sure that Maria would be found somewhere inside this castle.

He steered straight for the island, and when the boat bobbed right up against the castle walls he looked through the magic eye once more. Now he could see through the walls to a gigantic room, where his father was held, chained to a stone pillar in the middle, and where the sea witch stood, holding little Maria in her arms. A blazing charcoal-fire burned so brightly that Sancho could almost feel its warmth. To his horror, the sea witch seemed about to throw Maria on the fire.

He quickly pulled out all the hairs left in the cow's

tail, and put them in his pocket. He used one to help him get into the castle, for it turned into a rope-ladder which helped him climb over the walls. He found an open window and jumped into the big room, startling the witch so much that she dropped Maria, who at once ran across to her father, sobbing with fright.

"Who are you? What do you want?" hissed the witch.

"I've come for my father and my sister," cried Sancho, and, rushing towards her, tripped her up so that she fell headlong at his feet.

Another hair from the cow's tail turned into a strong cord, which he used to truss the witch up as his mother trussed up chickens for cooking. Then he untied his father and comforted the crying Maria.

"Let us get away from here," said Sancho. "The witch may work her way free."

Joaquin had been tied to the pillar so long that he was almost as stiff as the stone itself.

"How ever did you find us?" he began, but Sancho knew there was no time to tell him the whole story.

The huge room seemed to have no way out except the window which Sancho had used. It was high in the wall, however, and neither Joaquin nor Maria would be able to climb out to safety that way. So Sancho once again looked through the magic eye and saw that inside the stone pillar was a spiral staircase leading downward. He found its secret door, and opened it wide. First he seized the sea witch, who struggled like a wild thing, but was powerless to prevent him throwing her right the way down.

Then the three of them ran downstairs, round and round and round until they were quite giddy. At the bottom they saw the sea witch, and they were relieved to notice she was quite dead.

"Look, Sancho," said his father. "Look over there. All those chests full of precious gems. They must be the witch's treasure store."

Ranged neatly at the bottom of the staircase were many sea chests, their lids unable to close properly because they were crammed with jewels.

"Let us fill our pockets with them; when we are home again we shall be rich," said Sancho, taking command.

"Shall we really go home?" echoed Joaquin, hardly able to believe it. "I thought I should never see you both again, and Dolores your mother."

"Mother is well," said Sancho, rather impatiently. "Let us hurry, father, you need food and rest."

The stairway gave place to an underground road, and at the end of this road they smelt the fresh air once more. It brought them out under the castle walls to a little sandy beach. There was no sign of the skin boat, but in its place a handsome painted boat with sails and comfortable seats for the passengers was waiting.

"Where is the crew?" asked Joaquin, for nobody could be seen.

"I've learnt not to ask questions," said Sancho. "It is more of the russet cow's magic!"

His father looked very questioningly at him, but he was too tired to puzzle it out, and hardly had he stretched out in the boat before he was fast asleep. Maria, too, soon slept. Only Sancho remained awake, marvelling how the boat with its unseen crew kept a steady course, and covered mile after mile no matter which way the wind blew.

At last even Sancho fell asleep, and nobody woke up until they were by the very beach where Sancho and Maria had been playing. Of course, it was all strange to Joaquin, for he had never seen their new home. But Dolores was on the beach, collecting shell-fish, and when she saw them she wept for joy. She helped them out of the boat, and kept touching them in turn, hardly able to believe they were really alive.

Sancho, however, could not forget his dear russet cow, and how, in order to save his father and Maria, he had been forced to kill her. The least he could do was to return to the last place where she had spoken to him and say his thanks. To his surprise, the skin boat came floating over the water, and came to rest at his feet.

"Dear russet cow," said Sancho, with a lump in his throat as he remembered her kindness, "you were the best friend any boy could ask for. How I wish you were still alive and well!"

He decided to give her a good burial, and collected

her skin, eyes, and some bones which were still on the beach. Then he felt something sticking into him. It was the very last hair from the cow's tail, which had become stuck in the lining of his pocket. He pulled it out and threw it on top of the pile.

At that very moment there was a flash of lightning and the russet cow sprang to her feet, as sleek and well as she had ever been. Sancho patted her and stroked her, and nuzzled his face against her side, telling her how good and clever she was. But the cow just looked at him and never said a word.

Then Sancho led her home, and told his mother and father the whole story from beginning to end.

"With these jewels we found in the sea witch's castle I can buy a good farm and we can live well for the rest of our lives," said Joaquin. "As for the russet cow, she shall live as one of the family. Nothing shall be too good for her, because our safety and our good fortune are due to her."

And so it was, and the russet cow lived to a very great age. But she never spoke again.

The Girl who turned to Stone

IN A VILLAGE near the mountains there lived a cacique who had a very pretty daughter. She was as good as she was beautiful, and since her mother's death had lived quietly in her father's house, which was the best in the village for the cacique (the English form is cazique) is a local chief. Now, one day her father left home to attend a big celebration some distance away, where he met a handsome woman whom he took home for his new wife.

The daughter did not like her stepmother, for she believed that behind her mask of fine manners she was a cold and cruel woman. The cacique had no idea of this, and hoped that his wife would prove a second mother to his daughter. Unhappily, the stepmother became very jealous of the girl's beauty and secretly hated her because of it.

Not long afterwards the cacique arranged a marriage between his daughter and the son of a neighbouring cacique. The young couple made a handsome pair, and every one said life was sure to bring them happiness. Preparations for the grandest wedding in the district were begun. The stepmother pretended to be happy, too, but actually she felt more and more angry to see how the girl's beauty increased as the wedding day grew nearer. The stepmother began to spend every waking moment in schemes to prevent the marriage.

One night she stole out of the village without being seen. She visited a sorceress, a woman who was feared by the Indians because of her knowledge and her power of enchantment.

She spread some gifts out on the ground in front of the witch.

"Help me, O wise one," she begged. "Give me something that will make my stepdaughter so ugly that nobody will want to marry her!"

The sorceress asked some questions about the girl and her life, and then told the other woman to return in four days' time.

"By that time I can promise you what you ask," she said, "but, of course, such magic is not to be had for nothing."

By this she meant that she wanted more presents, and the stepmother eagerly agreed. It was hard to live through the next few days at home, keeping a false face to every one who spoke about the wedding that was to be, but the stepmother hugged to her heart the terrible secret of the harm she planned to the girl.

Promptly at the appointed time she returned to the sorceress's dwelling. Here the witch had prepared a tiny stone jar full of a thick, white cream.

"Be careful with it, for it is the strongest enchantment I know," warned the witch. "It will turn flesh to stone, and yours as quickly as hers."

The stepmother took the cream, and gave a second lot of gifts to the sorceress. Then she went happily home, waiting her chance until the night before the wedding. When every one in the house was sleeping, and the bride soundest of all, the stepmother crept into the girl's room and smeared the magic cream upon her face. The girl did not wake up, and the stepmother went away without having been seen.

The day of the wedding itself was one of noise and bustle from the very earliest hour, with guests arriving from every house for miles around. The stepmother wore her finest clothes and looked very handsome, but, of course, everybody was waiting to see the bride, and to judge for themselves if she were really as beautiful as gossip said.

Alas! when the girl appeared there was a gasp of horror from the crowd. She, too, wore her finest clothes, but her face, which had always won her so many admirers, now made people shudder with dismay, for it was hard and blank as stone.

Frightened, she turned to her father.

"Why do they look away? What have I done to them?" she asked.

Even her devoted father could hardly bear to look into her face, so sadly changed was it.

"Father, tell me what is the matter," she cried in despair, but the cacique could only shake his head. He could not find the words to tell her.

The stepmother suddenly began to weep noisily, and covered her eyes with one hand, as if to show she could no longer stand the sight of the girl. But the cacique noticed that one of her fingers was stone, exactly the same as his daughter's face.

Almost blind with rage, he dragged his wife indoors, and there made her confess what she had done. A drop of cream on the tip of her finger, when she rubbed it on the girl's face, had led to her discovery.

The cacique called in the village machi, who was also a sorcerer, but who used his magic powers to do good.

"I cannot be sure that I can undo such powerful enchantment," he said, and when he had carefully examined the girl he knew he was powerless.

"Here is the rest of the cream my wife used," said the cacique. "Can't you use it to find a remedy?"

The machi took the cream, and later on visited the same sorceress that the stepmother had gone to, and asked her to give him a cure.

"It is impossible," said the sorceress. "The cream was made from the bones of a dead man. To cure the girl all these bones must be found. But it will not be easy, for they were scattered to the four winds."

The machi returned to the village, and told the girl

and the cacique what had to be done. Naturally there was no question of a wedding now, and the future husband and guests went back to their villages. The cacique refused to speak another word to his wife, and had her put to death as a punishment for her cruelty. This, however, did nothing to make the unhappy daughter better, and at last she decided she must leave the village altogether.

Her father was broken-hearted.

"I have no wife now," he said, "if you leave me I shall have no daughter either."

The girl sighed.

"Dear father," she said gently, "I do not want to leave you, but you have seen how my face frightens the villagers. It will spoil your life too if I stay here. Let me live in the forest and mountains, where nobody will see me. At least the birds and the animals are not afraid."

So the girl went away, and lived like a wanderer in the forest. She lived on nuts of the hazel-tree and the cinnamon, on berries from the myrtles and the *ngevuñ* creeper, on the *pehuen*, the floury cone of the monkey-puzzle-tree, which grows wild in those forests, and on mushrooms and wild potatoes. She had companions wherever she went, for the animals of the forest knew she would never harm them, and she would talk to them and look on them as her friends.

One day she came to the banks of a river and, being tired and thirsty, knelt down to drink. Her eyes, close to the water, glimpsed a tiny ant struggling for its life against the current which threatened to sweep it away into midstream. Pitying the little creature, she picked a long blade of grass and tossed it into the river. The ant climbed on to it and reached safety. It fanned its wings in the sunshine to dry them, and then flew four times round the girl's head, crying, "Dig, dig," before flying away out of sight.

The girl loosened the earth at her feet and disclosed some gleaming white bones.

"There must be some reason why the ant told me to find these bones," she said to herself, and placed them carefully in a bag.

Some days later, as she was walking alongside a stream, she came upon a toad which was about to be swallowed by a snake. Her foot pressed hard upon a dry twig, which broke with a sharp noise that startled the snake, and gave the toad time to jump away. The snake slithered away and was seen no more, but the toad leaped four times in the air in front of the girl, croaking as it did so, "Dig, dig," and then vanished into the undergrowth at the side of the stream.

Obediently the girl loosened the earth at her feet, feeling expectantly now for more bones, and she was not disappointed. Soon she had a few more to add to her collection in the bag.

On she went until she arrived at the shores of a deep lake, where she found a young deer, bleeding almost to death with wounds caused by sharp arrows that

were still piercing its flesh. Her eyes filled with tears at the suffering of the pretty animal, and as she drew out each arrow with great care her tears washed away the blood. She cleansed the wounds, and after a while the deer was able to stand, shakily at first, then more strongly. It gazed at her, murmuring, "Dig, dig," and moved gracefully away.

For the third time the girl dug in the ground at her feet, and once more found some white bones, which she put in the bag with the others.

"I wonder if I have enough?" she said, and assembled the bones neatly on the ground. It was clear she had a complete skeleton except for the head.

"Perhaps I shall be told where to find the head," she said, and the thought gave her courage to continue her wanderings.

A few days later, on a path that led into the mountains, she came upon a puma, which was thrashing its tail and roaring with pain. One paw was badly swollen, and the girl saw that a thorn had driven its way deep into the pad, and that the surrounding flesh was poisoned. When the puma saw her it became quiet, and gave a beseeching look, asking for help.

She conquered her fear, and went boldly up to the animal. The thorn was so deep in the puma's paw that she had to bend down and pull it out with her teeth. As she did so the poison spurted out, the swelling disappeared quickly, and the puma was soon well again. It licked the girl's face, and she could have cried for joy, for here at least was a living thing that was not afraid of her face of stone. The puma led her into its cave, and brought her fresh drinking-water, carrying it in a skull between its jaws.

The girl sipped the water, and wondered if this skull could be the last missing piece of her skeleton. She arranged the bones, and the skull fitted them perfectly. As she put the last piece in position a stray thorn pricked her finger so that a drop of red blood fell on the bones. That very instant the skeleton sprang to life before her eyes, becoming a smiling young man, happy to have been released from his enchantment.

He stepped forward to kiss her in gratitude, and his

embrace restored her face of stone to all its former beauty.

There was nothing to stop them returning to the villages in the valley, but the girl had grown fond of her wild, free life, and could not forget how cruelly she had been treated. As for the young man, he was willing to live wherever the girl decided, so they stayed in the mountains, living as they pleased, and guarded for as long as it lived by the faithful puma.

The Princess and the Riddle

THERE WAS once a king who had an only daughter. She was very beautiful and very clever, and her father believed there was no one in the country who could match her. He declared that if any man could compose a riddle which the Princess could not solve within one day, then that man had his permission to marry the Princess and become heir to the throne. But if a man composed a riddle which the Princess could guess within the allotted time, then that unhappy man would forfeit his life.

In spite of this risk, young men from all corners of the kingdom flocked to court, eager to try their luck. Each one failed, and each one had his head cut off the following noon.

Now far away on a tiny farm lived a young man called Tiburce. He was not handsome and he was not clever, and his mother often wondered how he would get on when she was dead and could no longer look after him, for she was his only living relative. One day

Tiburce told his mother he had decided to go to court and make up a riddle for the Princess.

In vain his mother wept and pleaded with him. She was sure he was not clever enough to make up a riddle that the Princess could not solve.

But Tiburce was very determined, and his mother, certain that he would meet a horrible death at the royal palace after the Princess guessed his riddle, planned to prevent this. She baked some *tortillas*, flat little cakes which Tiburce liked, adding a painless and tasteless poison to them. She expected her son to eat them when he camped for the night on his way to the palace, and hoped the poison would bring him a merciful and peaceful death while he was asleep.

Tiburce groomed his donkey, thanked his mother for the *tortillas*, and said good-bye. He could not understand why she cried so bitterly.

"Cheer up, mother," he said kindly; "you are crying so much that anyone would think you never expected to see me again!"

Since this was exactly what his mother was thinking, only she could not tell him so, she began to cry harder than ever. At last Tiburce shook his head in bewilderment, mounted his donkey, and rode away.

When dusk fell he looked round for a quiet spot to pass the night. He was so tired that he did not bother to eat anything, but simply lay down on the ground and fell asleep at once. His donkey, however, nosed around until it found the *tortillas*, which it gobbled up greedily. Then the donkey too fell asleep, but, alas! it was a sleep from which it never awakened.

Next morning, when he sat up, yawning and blinking in the bright light, Tiburce was amazed to see that his donkey had died peacefully in the night. Indeed, four black birds of prey were already sitting on the donkey, tearing away at its flesh. Tiburce rubbed his eyes to make sure that he was not still dreaming, and was even more surprised to see that one by one the birds rolled over on the ground, dead as door-nails.

He picked the birds up, tied them together by the feet, and slung them over his shoulder. Then he set off down the road, resolved to finish his journey even if he had to walk all the way to the royal city.

He had hardly gone more than a hundred yards when a band of seven robbers appeared, and with black looks and angry shouts demanded his money and his food. Tiburce turned his pockets inside out to show he had no money at all, and, now that the *tortillas* were eaten, he had no food either. The robbers were disappointed and angry, for they had not eaten for two days, and they were very hungry indeed. They snatched the dead birds which Tiburce still carried over his shoulder, plucked their feathers, and cooked them quickly over a wood-fire.

By this time Tiburce was very hungry too, and the birds smelt good as they roasted.

"Kind sirs," he began timidly, "I gave you the

birds. I hope you will remember that when you come to divide up the food."

The robbers laughed loudly at the mere idea.

"If you have money to pay for your supper you can have some," they said, and laughed loudly again at such a good joke.

Since Tiburce had no money, as the robbers knew, he did not think it a good joke at all, and sat a little to one side, trying not to smell the appetising aroma of roast fowl. The robbers did not even look at him as they ate up every scrap. There was nothing at all left for Tiburce, and the robbers soon fell asleep.

At first they snorted and snored in their sleep, but presently everything was still and silent. Tiburce, puzzled by a feeling of strangeness, crept cautiously over to the robbers, and was astonished to see they were all dead. He went from one to the other, but every one of the seven was dead.

"The air must be very bad in these parts," said Tiburce to himself; "the sooner I get away the better."

He was still hungry, and just at that moment he saw a dove flying back to her nest in the tree-tops. He seized the rifle of one of the dead robbers and aimed at the dove. He missed the bird but dislodged her nest, which fell to the ground, with eggs inside it still unbroken.

"Well, then, I must make do with the eggs, if I cannot have the bird," said Tiburce.

He took a book from one of the robbers to make a fire, and cooked the eggs in the embers. After eating he marched down the road, crossed a river by a foot-bridge, and at last came to the royal palace. Here he told the doorkeeper he wished to try for the hand of the Princess.

The doorkeeper laughed to see such a dusty, shabby young man, but Tiburce took no notice.

"Every one has a right to ask the Princess a riddle, isn't that so?" he asked.

"Yes, young man," agreed the doorkeeper. "But do you know how many have lost their lives because the Princess guessed their riddles? She is the cleverest young lady in the land."

However, Tiburce insisted on being taken to see the King and the Princess, and he was led up to the throne. The courtiers laughed and nudged each other as they pointed at Tiburce's ragged clothes and wind-roughened skin.

"Tell the Princess your riddle," commanded the King. "She will spend the night solving it, and if by to-morrow morning she has guessed rightly you will pay with your life. If, however, she cannot guess your riddle she will become your wife and you shall become king after me."

So Tiburce took a deep breath and recited his riddle.

> "I left home: I left on my donkey.
> A dead donkey killed four creatures.
> These four killed seven.
> I aimed at what I saw,
> But I killed what I did not see.
> I ate meat which was not yet born,
> And I cooked it with words."

The Princess listened carefully to the riddle and then went to her rooms to try to puzzle out its meaning. She stayed awake all night, thinking, but Tiburce slept soundly in the finest bed he had ever seen in his life.

Next morning every one was in the throne-room waiting to hear about the riddle. The Princess was brought in and solemnly asked if she could explain it. To every one's surprise, she shook her head. The riddle was too hard for the cleverest girl in the kingdom, and a simple country lad had made it up. The Princess could not help stamping her foot in anger. It would not have been so bad if Tiburce had been clever and handsome, but he looked so ordinary, and he was not even a prince!

But the King had given his word, and the Princess had to fight back her annoyance. When the wedding-day came Tiburce was wearing a fine set of clothes, and really looked almost as splendid as a real prince.

As for Tiburce's mother, when news came that her son was not dead after all, but was actually going to marry the Princess and be the next King, she could hardly believe her ears. But, being a wise mother, she simply smiled and said nothing. And of all the people in the kingdom Tiburce's mother was the only one who really guessed what the riddle meant.

The Old Man and the Beanstalk

In a certain village there lived a poor old man and his wife. They had no money and no family to look after them. Sometimes they were so hungry that they had to beg for food from their neighbors. One day the poor old man went to a farmer to ask for bread.

"The harvest is bad and I have nothing to spare," said the farmer, "but I have some beans left over from the planting. Take them and sow them yourself. Later on you will be able to sell the crop at market."

The old man thanked the farmer and took the seeds home to his wife. They both felt disappointed with the farmer's gift, for they did not believe the beans would grow. However, they dug a trench in the ground, dropped the beans in it, covered them with earth, and watered them well. Then they left the patch of cleared earth and forgot all about the beans.

But the plants grew and grew in a mysterious fashion. Every day they grew taller and stronger, unlike any other kind of bean in the district. Soon their topmost leaves were higher than houses. When the old couple happened to pass that way they were astonished to see how the plants had grown.

"They are very special beans," said the old man to his wife, "and I will look after them well. When they are harvested such unusual beans will fetch a good price at the market."

So every day they visited the beans, tended them carefully, and sighed with pride as they watched them grow. Now the plants were so tall that they towered into the sky and their tips were hidden. Yet no flowers or beans could be seen, and the old woman became very scornful.

"How are you going to sell the beans at the market, when there are no flowers growing to form the fruit?" she asked.

Her husband had no answer to this, but hoped that if they were patient all would be well.

"There are not even any flower buds to be seen," grumbled his wife. "Let us chop it down and sell the stalks for firewood. Look, they are as thick as saplings already."

But her husband felt that so noble a plant should be worth more than firewood, and he had become proud of this strange crop of beans. Day after day they argued bitterly about what to do, and finally the old man decided to climb up the biggest beanstalk and ask God for His advice. He pretended to his wife that he was going away begging, but when she was not looking he began to climb up the plant. Branch by branch he went until he arrived at the gates of Heaven.

Here he gave a loud shout, so that St Peter came to see what was the matter. The old man told St Peter his troubles, and St Peter went to God and repeated the whole story. Then God told St Peter to give the old man a special ring which would grant his wishes, but only on condition that the wishes were sensible ones. If he wished for anything foolish the ring would lose its particular power.

The old man took the ring, promised to be sensible about it, gave heartfelt thanks for this gift, and climbed back down the beanstalk.

Meanwhile his wife, finding that her husband had been away from home for two whole days and one night, had made up her mind that he was dead, and she stayed indoors, mourning the fact that she was now alone.

When her husband reached the door of his home he rubbed his new ring and said, "Magic ring, gift of God, I wish for a new suit of clothes and a fine pair of shoes."

Immediately they appeared on the ground before him. He put them on, and then knocked at his front door. But he looked so rich and important in his new clothes that at first his wife thought he was a stranger. She began to tremble in case this unknown man had come to turn her out of her home.

"Don't be afraid," he said. "It's me. Don't you recognize me? Let me in, and I will tell you everything that has happened."

As soon as she understood everything the old woman was eager to test the ring for herself, and they asked for all kinds of things, all very useful, like clothes, furniture, and blankets, with plenty of good food and wine.

To show his gratitude to God, the old man began to go regularly to church. He took his ring with him, for he feared that in his absence his wife might ask for some foolish wish to be granted. Each time he left the ring for safe keeping with the wise woman of the village, who lived next to the church.

However, he had made the mistake of letting her see how valuable he considered the ring, and she began to wonder what was so special about it. She held it in her hand and twisted it one way and then the other.

"Are you a magic ring?" she asked. "If so, bring me a new dress!"

To her joy, a new dress at once appeared on the table.

"Now I've found you, I'm going to keep you," she said, and found a ring of her own which was very similar in appearance. When the old man came out of church and called for his ring she gave him the false one.

Of course, as soon as he reached home and asked the ring to provide a meal he realized that he had been tricked and given a different ring. Purple with rage, he rushed back to the wise woman, demanding his own ring back.

She pretended to know nothing whatever about it, and as he was a little afraid of her and did not want to make her into his enemy he did nothing more about it.

"Give me food for a journey," he said to his wife. "I am going to climb the beanstalk again."

Up and up he went, branch after branch, climbing until he came to the gates of Heaven, where St Peter stood waiting.

"And what do you want now?" asked St Peter.

"Give me a tablecloth which will be covered with food when I spread it on the table," begged the old man.

So St Peter gave him a tablecloth which would always be covered with food when it was unfolded. The same condition applied to the use of the tablecloth as had applied to the use of the ring—he was not to expect any extravagant banquet.

The old man thanked St Peter for the gift, and went back home, where he and his wife enjoyed their first good supper for several days.

Next day he set out for church as usual, and again

stopped at the wise woman's house to leave the tablecloth with her for safe keeping.

"Be sure not to unfold it or harm will befall you," he warned her.

But, of course, the wise woman did not believe a word of what he said, and she could hardly wait for him to leave her house so that she could unfold it and see what happened. Immediately it became covered with good food, and the wise woman smiled cunningly. She took out of a cupboard a tablecloth of her own, very similar in appearance to the magic one, and when the old man called in to collect it she gave him the false tablecloth.

Once again the old man knew he had been tricked as soon as he reached his home and unfolded the tablecloth, for nothing at all happened.

"Give me food for a journey," he ordered his wife, "for I must climb up the beanstalk again."

So for the third time the old man began the weary climb up and up, branch by branch, until he reached the gates of Heaven. St Peter was already there, patiently waiting to listen to the old man's troubles.

"Choose your last magic thing," said St Peter, showing the old man a host of objects. "But be sure you make a good choice, for this must be the very last one."

The old man chose a magical bundle of sticks, tied up in a parcel. Down the beanstalk he climbed, and was very tired indeed when he reached home, but

early next morning he was up and ready to go to church. On his way he stopped at the wise woman's house and left his parcel with her.

"Be sure not to say, 'Come out, bundle of sticks,' or harm will befall you," he warned the woman.

But, of course, she did not believe a word of it, for when he had said the same thing about the tablecloth, and she had unfolded it, no harm had come her way. Quite the reverse, for she had been given food and wine. So as soon as he had gone she took the parcel, and cried, "Come out, bundle of sticks."

At once the whole room seemed filled with tiny, needle-like sticks, with sharp points, which darted towards the wise woman, stinging her until she cried for mercy. But, alas! there was nobody to hear her cries until the old man returned from church.

"Before I help you tell me what you have done with my magic ring and my magic tablecloth," he demanded sternly.

Still crying with pain, she told him where to find them. Then the sticks became quiet and fell one by one into a neat pile, so that they could be packed away in their parcel again. The old man took away his magic gifts and never again let them out of his sight. He and his wife were careful to behave sensibly, and they never lacked food or warmth for the rest of their lives.

The Little Tenca and the Snowflake

THE TENCA is a song-bird that can be found in Southern Chile. It is not very big, but it sings sweetly and is much loved. One year a little tenca hatched her family late in the year, so that it was winter when the fledglings came out of the shell. The tenca looked after them well, flying out for food each day, and when the baby birds were well fed she would sit on the nest, keeping them warm under her wings. When she was away, looking for food, the fledglings would snuggle down together for comfort against the sleet and biting winds.

One day the little tenca was still a long way from her nest, searching for food, when she was caught in a sudden snowstorm. Thick white snow flurried round her, settling on her glossy feathers, slipping over her yellow bill. It was like trying to fly through a thick woollen blanket, and the tenca dropped to the ground and tried to hop along, buffeted from side to side. As she was doing so she stumbled against a snow-drift and hurt her foot on a snowflake.

"Snow, snow," asked the little tenca sadly, "why are you unkind to me, hurting my foot?"

But the snow replied, "Don't blame me. It's the sun's fault making me melt."

So the little tenca flew above the storm, right up to the sun and asked sadly, "Sun, sun, why are you unkind to me, melting the snow, so that the snow burns my foot?"

But the sun only shone more brightly and replied, "Don't blame me. It's the cloud's fault for hiding my rays."

So the tenca flew off to the cloud and asked sadly, "Cloud, cloud, why are you unkind to me, hiding the sun's rays, for the sun melts the snow, and the snow burns my foot?"

But the cloud scudded across the sky, saying, "Don't blame me. It's the wind's fault for chasing me."

So the tenca went to the home of the wind, and asked sadly, "Wind, wind, why are you unkind to me, chasing the cloud, for it hides the sun's rays, and the sun melts the snow, and the snow burns my foot?"

But the wind whistled merrily and said, "Don't blame me. It's the wall's fault for standing in my way."

Then the tenca flew down to the wall and asked sadly, "Wall, wall, why are you unkind to me,

standing in the wind's way, for it chases the cloud, that hides the sun's rays, that melt the snow, and the snow burns my foot?"

But the wall stood up straight and said, "Don't blame me. It's the mouse's fault for making a hole in me."

So the tenca hopped away to find the mouse and asked sadly, "Mouse, mouse, why are you unkind to me, making a hole in the wall, for the wall stands in the way of the wind, that chases the cloud, which hides the sun's rays, which melt the snow and the snow burns my foot?"

But the mouse squeaked, "Don't blame me. It's the cat's fault for chasing me."

So the tenca flew off to find the cat and asked sadly, "Cat, cat, why are you unkind to me, chasing the mouse, that makes a hole in the wall, for the wall stands in the way of the wind, which chases the cloud, that hides the sun's rays, which melt the snow, and the snow burns my foot?"

But the cat only washed its face and said, "Don't blame me. It's the dog's fault for running after me."

The tenca went off to find the dog and asked sadly, "Dog, dog, why are you unkind to me, running after the cat, which chases the mouse, which makes a hole in the wall, for the wall stands in the way of the wind, which chases the cloud, that hides the sun's rays, that melt the snow, and the snow hurts my foot?"

But the dog scampered away, and said as it went, "Don't blame me. It's the stick's fault for beating me."

The tenca flew away to find the stick and asked sadly, "Stick, stick, why are you unkind to me, beating the dog, that chases the cat, which runs after the mouse, which makes a hole in the wall, for the wall stands in the way of the wind, that chases the cloud, which hides the sun's rays, that melt the snow, and the snow burns my foot?"

But the stick only said, "Don't blame me. It's the fire's fault for burning me."

So the tenca went to the fire and asked sadly, "Fire, fire, why are you unkind to me, burning the stick, that hits the dog, that chases the cat, which runs after the mouse, which makes a hole in the wall, for the wall stands in the way of the wind, that chases the cloud, which hides the sun's rays, that melt the snow, and the snow burns my foot?"

But the fire flared and hissed as it said, "Don't blame me. It's the water's fault for putting me out."

So the tenca flew on until she came to the water, and she said sadly, "Water, water, why are you unkind to me, putting out the fire, that burns the stick, which hits the dog, that chases the cat, which runs after the mouse, that makes a hole in the wall, for the wall stands in the way of the wind, which chases the cloud, that hides the sun's rays, which melt the snow, and the snow burns my foot?"

Then the water gurgled and said, "Don't blame me. It's the ox's fault for drinking me."

The tenca flew away to the ox and asked sadly, "Ox, ox, why are you unkind to me, drinking the water, which puts out the fire, that burns the stick, which beats the dog, that chases the cat, which runs after the mouse, that makes a hole in the wall, for the wall stands in the way of the wind, that chases the cloud, which hides the rays of the sun, that melt the snow, and the snow hurts my foot?"

But the ox only glanced up from his grazing and said, "Don't blame me. It's the knife's fault because it kills me."

The tenca began to feel tired, but off she flew to

find the knife and asked sadly, "Knife, knife, why are you so unkind to me, killing the ox, which drinks the water, that puts out the fire, which burns the stick, that beats the dog, which chases the cat, which runs after the mouse, that makes a hole in the wall, for the wall stands in the way of the wind, that chases the cloud, which hides the rays of the sun, that make the snow melt, and the snow burns my foot?"

But the knife flashed in the bright light and said, "Don't blame me. It's the man's fault for making me."

So the tenca flew straight to the man and asked sadly, "Man, man, why are you unkind to me, making the knife, that kills the ox, which drinks the water, that puts out the fire, that burns the stick, which beats the dog, which chases the cat, that runs after the mouse, which makes a hole in the wall, for the wall stands in the way of the wind, which chases the cloud, that hides the rays of the sun, that melt the snow, and the snow hurts my foot?"

And the man said, "Ask God Who created me."

So the tired little tenca flew on, up, up, up in the heavens until she came to the Throne of God. She bent her head until her beak touched the ground and asked bravely, "Lord God, please tell me why you created Man? For man made the knife, which killed the ox, that drank the water, which put out the fire, that burnt the stick, which beat the dog, that chased the cat, which ran after the mouse, which made a hole in the wall, and the wall stood in the way of the wind, that chased the cloud, which hid the rays of the sun, that melted the snow, and the snow burnt my foot."

Then the tenca was overcome by exhaustion and misery and lay on the ground, her wings drooping, her eyes dull with pain, so that every one pitied her.

And God, touched by the tenca's grief, said gently, "Now, now, little tenca, be brave. Fly back to your babies; they are cold and hungry."

The tenca, like a good Christian, obeyed at once, and by the time she alighted on the edge of her own nest again she saw that her foot, which had been burned, was now perfectly healed.

The Magic Ring

THERE WAS once an old Indian widow who had three sons. They were all very poor, and when the sons grew up they determined to leave home to seek their fortune, and bring their mother some money to comfort her in her old age. One day the two elder sons rode off together, saying, "We shall go and find work," but the youngest son went a different way and said nothing.

He soon reached the sea, but found nothing there of value except a pretty cockleshell, which he put in his pocket. When he returned home his brothers were already back, with plenty of money, which they had earned in the town.

"What have you brought?" they asked him scornfully.

When he showed his cockleshell they beat him over the head, saying the shell was worthless. Sadly the youngest brother set off on his travels once more, his pockets entirely empty except for the shell.

He journeyed for two or three days without seeing any person and without finding anything to eat. At last he was ready to faint with hunger. He took the cockleshell out of his pocket and prised it open with a sharp stone, meaning to eat the meat inside. But the shell was full of sand, and he threw it down in disgust so that it fell and broke into pieces. Then the Indian saw something that glittered in the dust. It was a silver ring, with a single bright stone. He slipped it on his finger, and it fitted perfectly.

Dusk was falling, and he was so tired that he curled up by the side of the road and fell instantly asleep. He was awakened by the sound of horse's hoofs, and saw two men riding together on one heavily laden horse. They did not see him at first, so he moved quietly behind a rock, for they looked fierce and were well armed. Unfortunately he sneezed, the men looked round at once, and within seconds he had been found. They shook him roughly by the shoulder and demanded to know his business.

"I am only a poor Indian looking for work," he said. "I have no money, nothing worth taking."

As he said this he kept his hands behind his back, being afraid that they would see his ring and promptly steal it. To make doubly sure he turned the ring back to front, so that the bright stone did not show. The moment he did so he heard one man say to the other, "Where has that rascal disappeared to?"

By what they said and did, the Indian gathered

that they could not see him, and he wondered if they had suddenly gone blind. He danced in front of them, but still they could not see him. He went over to their horse, which stood laden with a heavy sack full of gold and silver, and pushed the saddle off.

The two men, who were professional robbers, saw their saddle fall to the ground, apparently for no reason at all, and they trembled with fear.

"Can it be Pillan, god of thunder, playing tricks on us?" they muttered, frightened.

The young Indian picked up a stick and, before the robbers knew what was happening, knocked them senseless, then mounted their horse and rode off, taking the sack of gold and silver with him. He did not stop for anything until he reached home, where he went indoors and proudly gave his mother the sack of gold and silver.

A few moments later his elder brothers returned home, where the sight of so much treasure on their mother's table made them jealous, and they tried to take it for themselves. The youngest brother quickly turned his magic ring around and became invisible. His brothers thought they must be dreaming. Before they could recover their wits the youngest son mounted his horse and rode away.

A few days later he returned with some money, although he expected to find his mother living in comfort because of the treasure he had brought her. To his anger, he found that his brothers had taken away all her money. She was as poor as ever.

"You shall not live here any longer," he said. "We'll go where my brothers cannot find you."

He took her to another district, found a tiny house for her, left her with some money, and rode away again to seek his fortune.

He rode deep into the mountains until he came to a great cave guarded by a huge animal with seven heads and seven tails. The monster growled and roared and prepared to spring, but the Indian turned his ring around and became invisible. He slew the animal, and cut off each head and each tail. A man and a woman sprang alive and well from each head and each tail. They were Indians whom the monster had caught and eaten.

With much rejoicing these people took their rescuer to their own village, which was on the plain near the sea. Their families and friends were glad to see them, for they had long ago been given up for lost. The young man was naturally the hero of the village.

He noticed that the prettiest girl in the village was also the saddest. She told him that her father, the cacique, had been taken the night before in an enchanted boat, manned by strange men who possessed only one leg between them all. This magic boat, a caleuche, came every moonless night, and if anyone were walking along the beach at that time there was every chance he would be kidnapped by this terrifying crew.

"Don't cry," said the young Indian, "to-night I will watch for this magic boat. We'll see what they do to *me*!"

There was no moon, and the dark sky seemed to melt into the dark sea. Soon he saw the outline of a black boat. It raced swiftly over the water like a skater on ice. The young man closed his eyes, pretending to be asleep. The strange crew of the caleuche jumped out on to the beach, seized the Indian, tied him up in a sack, and lugged him back to their boat.

When they undid the sack, expecting to see their prisoner, the young Indian turned his magic ring around his finger and became invisible. The sailors were furious, especially their captain, and they hunted all over the boat, but could not find him.

Careful to remain invisible, the Indian now explored the boat thoroughly, and found a cage where some men and women were imprisoned. They told him they were kept there until the crew felt hungry, and then one of them would be chosen to be eaten.

"No one will be eaten again, I promise you," said the Indian, and he waited until the crew of the caleuche were asleep, and then he cut off their heads, one by one. When they were all quite dead he opened the prisoners' cage and freed everybody. They chopped down the ship's masts and threw them into the sea to use as rafts.

The young Indian was the last to leave the caleuche, for he meant to burn it so that never again could it be a danger to the people of the mainland. He set light to it, but, being magic, it did not blaze up and then die away, but continued burning with a steady light. On moonless nights the caleuche can be seen burning still, and it means instant death to anyone who tries to put the fire out.

As for the young man, he swam safely to one of the rafts and reached shore with the others. Later on he married the cacique's pretty daughter. Her father was none the worse for having been a prisoner on the caleuche, but from that time onward on moonless nights he was very careful to stay at home.

Daughters of the Kalku

THERE ONCE lived a village sorcerer, or kalku, who had two daughters. Unlike the machi, who is a good witch, the kalku often uses his magic powers for his own selfish purposes, and many simple villagers fear him. Day by day the daughters grew more beautiful, and their father was well pleased.

"When they grow up I shall look out for two strong young men," he said to himself, "who will work for me in return for marrying my daughters."

When the girls were old enough to marry the kalku began to consider suitable husbands. At last his choice fell upon his two nephews. Besides being in the family already, they were strong and handsome, and would be able to work hard for their new father-in-law.

So he invited the young men, whose names were Konkel and Pediu, to visit him. The kalku welcomed them to his house and promised to give them his two daughters in marriage.

"But first," he warned them, "you must carry out a task to prove your worth."

"Certainly," agreed the brothers. "What do you want us to do?"

"Go and cut down my old trees," ordered the kalku, pointing to some sturdy oaks.

He gave each young man an axe, and told them to be sure to cut down the trees with a single blow of the axe. He believed this was an impossible task, for the axes were old and blunt.

Off went the young men, and when they came to the trees they tried to cut them down with a single blow of the axe, as the kalku had ordered. But the axes were useless against the hard, gnarled tree-trunks, and broke into pieces at the first blow. The brothers returned to the kalku and explained what had happened.

"From now on we will use our own axes," they promised, "and the job will be done."

"Very well," said the kalku, "you shall have one more chance."

Away went the brothers for the second time, and now they paused beneath the mightiest oak-tree of all. They gazed up through its branches at the blue sky, and called out to Pillan, the spirit who lives in the clouds. He commands the lightning and thunder, makes the volcanoes erupt and the land quiver with earthquakes. In addition, he is the lord of the axe, and the brothers knew that only he was powerful enough to help them.

"Send us down your fine axes, Pillan," they cried.

"Axes sharp enough to cut down the trees with a single blow. Help us, Pillan; listen to us."

Far up in the heavens came a noise like thunder. It was the sound of Pillan's axes crashing through the air. Four times the brothers cried out to Pillan, and each time they heard the axes coming nearer, until at their fourth cry the shining tools hurtled to the ground.

Konkel and Pediu each seized an axe, and chose an oak-tree. Pillan's axes cut through the tree-trunks like magic. After a single blow each tree fell shuddering to the ground. The task finished, the brothers returned to the kalku, who agreed to the two marriages.

A grand feast was celebrated by every one in the village, and the brothers settled down happily in their new home. Not long afterwards their father-in-law called them to him.

"Now that I have allowed you to marry my daughters, you must help me by hunting the wild bulls," he said.

"Very well," agreed the brothers, and they started off the next morning.

They reached the place where the wild bulls lived, and before nightfall had caught and killed every one. The kalku pretended to be pleased, but secretly he was surprised that the brothers were so clever, and determined to find a task so hard that the brothers could not possibly succeed. After they had failed he meant to make them work for him all the time as a punishment.

At last he hit upon a plan.

"Go and hunt my ostriches and my llamas," he ordered.

"Very well," answered the brothers, as usual, and once again they prepared to start the next morning.

The kalku sent his servant, a fox, to guide them to the spot where the ostriches and the llamas lived. The fox was sly and clever, wore shiny leather boots, and rode a black horse that galloped like the wind.

"What a fine horse you have," said the brothers, with some envy, for they had only one mule between them.

When they came to the place where the ostriches and llamas lived all three tried their luck at hunting them. The fox, mounted on his fine horse, spent the whole day chasing ostriches but could not catch one. At nightfall he left the young men there and went home to his master.

"Are the brothers still there?" demanded the kalku.

"Yes," said the fox, "they will not come home until they have carried out your orders."

Two days later the kalku told the fox to get news of the brothers. The fox went to their home, but the wives said they had not seen their husbands.

Not long afterwards the kalku sent his fox again to his daughters, and again there was the same reply.

The kalku then grew very angry. He thought the brothers had run away and would never return.

"Go at once to my daughters and kill them both," he told the fox.

The fox tried to find excuses so that he could avoid doing such a cruel deed.

"My foot hurts," he complained, hopping on one foot. "I am lame, I cannot walk."

"That's no reason," said the kalku crossly, "Go all the same, even if you have to walk slowly."

So the fox went off down the road, limping as if he had a wooden leg. However slowly he went, in the end he reached the house where the two wives lived, for it was not far away. Very sadly he obeyed his master's order and killed the two beautiful girls. They fell to the ground, where they lay quietly, as if asleep. Then the fox went home.

Not long afterwards the two brothers returned, having completed their task. When they went inside the house they were surprised to see that their wives appeared to be sleeping.

"What wicked wives!" they said to each other. "They should be up and about, cleaning the house and preparing a meal for us."

One of the brothers was so angry that he began to shake his wife, expecting to awaken her, but in a few minutes both young men saw there was something wrong. To their great sorrow, they realized that their beautiful wives were dead. They were so unhappy that they could think of nothing except to punish the kalku, for they knew he must be the cause of their wives' deaths.

"There is no time to be lost," said one.

"No," agreed the other. "Let us go at once and see that this wicked man pays for his crime."

The kalku was not at home, but the brothers found his servant, the fox, and they imprisoned him at once. Then, too sorrowful to let anything live, they each stretched an arm into the sky and pulled down the sun, which they placed in a cooking-pot with a lid over it.

"Let nothing alive remain on the earth!" they shouted angrily. "Let the night last for four years!"

Suddenly the air was filled with the sound of beating wings as every possible kind of bird came and fluttered round the brothers.

"Choose any one of our daughters for a wife," they begged, hoping to bring some happiness to the brothers so that the world might live again.

"Thank you," replied the brothers, "but your daughters are not like our own wives. We are sad because they have been killed, so we shall keep the sun shut up in the cooking-pot, and the night shall last four years."

The months passed in utter darkness. Many things died upon the earth, among them the kalku, but the brothers stubbornly refused to let the sun free. The birds longed to see the rosy dawn once more. One day the partridge had an idea.

"When the brothers go into their house I will hide beneath their mule," said he. "I shall wait until they are asleep, then I shall prod the mule until he jumps

around, and it should not be hard to get him to break the cooking-pot where the sun is hidden."

The plan worked perfectly. The pot was broken, and the sun climbed rapidly into the sky once more. Gradually all things began to live again, but the brothers stayed inside their house, mourning because their wives were dead. The sounds of their grief made every one feel sad.

Then the ostrich came to see them.

"What is the matter? Why do you weep all the time?" he asked.

"Our wives are dead," explained the brothers.

"Is that all?" asked the ostrich. "Listen carefully. Sing for me while I dance. Sing, 'Ostrich with the pierced nose, ostrich with the noisy mouth.' "

The ostrich scratched out a hole in the ground and began to dance rapidly, while the brothers chanted over and over again, "Ostrich with the pierced nose, ostrich with the noisy mouth." Round and round danced the ostrich, raising clouds of dust, and in the middle the brothers were surprised to see two old women appear.

"Don't stop singing," cried the ostrich, and it danced harder than ever.

"Ostrich with the pierced nose, ostrich with the noisy mouth," sang the brothers loudly, and now two young women appeared. They were beautiful, but each had only one eye.

"These are your wives," said the ostrich.

"So they are," replied Konkel and Pediu, very pleased.

Then the two old women gave an eye to each of the young ones, who became perfect living women again.

"Now perhaps you will be happy and stop weeping," said the ostrich, tired after so much dancing, and he sped quickly away into the darkness.

As for the young men, they had a second wedding feast and began to enjoy life once again.

The Strawberry Maid

MANY, MANY years ago by the shores of Lake Llanquihue there lived a race of giants who were so fierce and so ugly that they were feared for miles around. The people of the countryside kept as far away from the lake as they could, especially after dark, and when children were naughty their mothers would frighten them by saying, "Unless you are good, the King of the Giants will come for you and carry you off."

Now the King of the Giants was called Patancha, and one day he fell asleep in the warm sunshine by the edge of the lake. As soon as he was really deep in sleep he began to snore so heavily that the near-by trees shook and swayed as though caught in a terrible storm. All the birds stopped singing, took fright, and flew away. Only the other giants were not scared by the thunderous snoring of their King.

At the bottom of the lake itself lived some beautiful maidens, whose Queen, called the Strawberry Maid, was the loveliest of them all. The sound of the giant's snoring filtered down through the quiet water and puzzled them.

"Perhaps it is Pillan stirring," said the Strawberry Maid, "and a sign that we shall have a thunderstorm."

"Then we shall see the lightning streak through the water," said another of the girls. "But this is a strange sound for thunder."

"I have never heard it before," said another.

They became so curious that they decided to find out for themselves, and in no time at all they had swum up to the surface of the lake and waded along the shore to see what was the matter.

"Oh, look!" cried a girl. "It's one of those giants."

The Strawberry Maid peered closely at him.

"It's Patancha, too," she said, "the King of the Giants. Take care you do not wake him, for he might try to capture one of us."

Although the giant was fast asleep, he held a strange, magical object in his hand. It was a bright eye, set in a wheel, which spun endlessly round and round, for ever scanning the horizons. As it did so it sang in a shrill, whirring tone, "Be watchful, Patancha. Patancha, be watchful."

But, of course, Patancha was so fast asleep that he was not watchful at all.

Indeed, he snored more loudly than ever, and every now and then came an extra loud roar at which leaves dropped off the tree, and even some of the pebbles on the lake beach were dislodged and rolled down into the water. Used to the calm life under the lake, the maidens could hardly bear to hear such harsh, grating sounds, and first one, then another girl, picked up tiny pebbles and threw them at his nose, hoping that this tiny irritation would not be enough to wake him up completely but would stop the snoring.

But unhappily it had the opposite effect. A shower of little stones on his face did not hurt Patancha at all, for they felt hardly more than the weight of an insect alighting briefly on his cheek. He snored even worse than before, his entire body shaking with the fury of his snoring, so that the pebbles bounced off him, flying in all directions.

At this the lake maidens grew frightened at what they had done, and turned to run to the safety of their underwater homes. It was only just in time, for Patancha awakened at that instant, and saw the maidens running away, their bright hair floating in the wind like petals, their warning cries to each other like the chatter of swift water over the rocks.

Only their Queen, the Strawberry Maid, was not able to run fast enough to escape capture. Patancha stretched, yawned, and without hurrying himself extended his long arm and imprisoned the unfortunate girl. She wept and struggled, but it was no use. The giant had no intention of letting her go, and without harming her in any way took her back to his cave, where he placed her in the care of an old witch.

"Guard her well, and see that she has anything she wants," he said. "But, whatever you do, do not let her escape. Or you will suffer for it if she does!"

"You can rely on me," said the old witch. "My, isn't she pretty! Not like our own girls!"

And here she gave a dreadful cackle of laughter which made the Strawberry Maid shiver with fright.

The giant went outside and took up a hollow tree which he kept especially as a ceremonial trumpet. He blew a mighty blast on this instrument, to summon the rest of the giants. They ran quickly to him, for this trumpet call was one of their most solemn signals. Patancha would never use it for some trivial matter.

They shouted at him in a discordant chorus, each at the top of his voice, and each determined to say his bit, even if his neighbor were also talking at the same time.

"Well, well, what is it? Tell us, we are all here. Why have you called us? We were busy, but we came at once. What is it—something good or something bad?"

Their voices echoed across the lake meadows, while down in their homes on the lake bed the maidens heard the confused rumble of the giants' voices and huddled together for protection, fearing that their Queen was in danger.

Patancha smiled at the giants. Although he meant his smile to be a kindly one, and after all it was not really his fault that he was so ugly, the fact remains that when he smiled it was as though a cloud passed over the sun.

"You all know the lake maidens," he began.

The others nodded and nudged each other. They all knew the lake maidens well by sight, for all of them had glimpsed the girls at one time or another. They were captivated by the charm, beauty and delicacy of the lake maidens, who provided such a contrast to their own womenfolk. It was one of the great tragedies of a giant's life that he was so fierce and ugly that no one except another giant would ever dream of marrying him.

"Well, then," continued Patancha, "I have captured the fairest of them all, their Queen, the Strawberry Maid, and she is at this very moment in my cave."

Here the giants broke out into exclamations of delight. To have one of these delightful maidens actually living among them was something undreamed of.

"But this is not all," continued Patancha. "I have decided that the Strawberry Maid is to be my bride, and we shall be married with all possible speed."

The giants agreed that this was a splendid idea, and they went away to make preparations for the wedding feast. Patancha returned to his cave to tell the Strawberry Maid what was to happen to her.

She cried inconsolably as she listened. She had no wish to marry anyone at all if it meant leaving her lovely lake kingdom, and certainly she had no wish whatever to marry a fierce, ugly giant.

"There are many treasures of mine under the lake,"

she said wistfully. "Will you take them in exchange for my freedom?"

At first Patancha refused even to think of the idea, for he had fallen deeply in love with her, and thought there was no price on earth high enough to make up for her loss. But the Strawberry Maid was very persuasive, and it appeared that she was also very rich. Patancha had always liked riches, and generally got his treasures by stealing from people. Finally, he said that although he did not think he would let her go, at least it could do no harm if he went down to the lake with her to look at her treasures. Then he would be able to decide if there was enough for her ransom.

The Strawberry Maid immediately led him to the edge of the water and called to her maidens. They swam to the surface, and welcomed her with joy, thinking she was about to return to them. She explained that she wanted her finest treasures brought up so that Patancha could look at them. At the same time she whispered that, whatever the giant said, she was going to try to escape.

The maidens began to distract Patancha's attention, diving for the lake treasures one by one. They appeared and disappeared so rapidly below the lake that the giant grew sadly confused. The Strawberry Maid awaited her opportunity, and when the giant was not looking she ran off to the water's edge and dived into its depths.

Patancha was suddenly aware that she had gone, and ran to the spot where she had been, but could not see her anywhere. As some consolation he found a canister of precious jewels where the maiden had last stood. He realized that he had lost his beautiful bride for ever. The Strawberry Maid would never return now. The jewels, handsome and valuable though they were, seemed a miserable substitute for the beauty he had lost.

With a cry of rage he picked up an enormous stone and hurled it at the centre of the lake, meaning to punish, if not the Strawberry Maid herself, then some of her maidens. But when the splashing ceased the waters became still, and nothing could be seen of any maiden. Baffled and unhappy, the giant went back to his cave, taking the jewels with him.

And from that day, it is said, that part of the lake has been marked by a great stone, which the villagers call the Big Stone—big enough for a giant. And in that district, too, the spring comes early and the summer lingers, and the strawberries grow as big as walnuts, and are still ripening and full of sweetness long after they are over in other parts of Chile.

The Story of the Chonchon

THERE WAS once a Mapuche Indian who lived happily with his two wives. The work of the home was shared between the two women equally, and if one of them wished to go out she left her own child in the care of the other wife. The husband worked all day in the fields, and at night stayed in the village drinking with his friends. Life was very peaceful, and the two wives got on together very well, so that the husband felt extremely satisfied with his double family.

Now, one night when the husband was still in the village, drinking as usual, one of the children woke up and began to cry. His persistent cries attracted the attention of the other mother, and she became alarmed in case the child were seriously ill.

"Try to sleep, little one," she said comfortingly. "Sleep now, and in the morning everything will seem better."

But the cries continued, and she wondered why its

real mother did not get up to look after her child. She crossed the room to see how she could still sleep when her child needed her, but when she reached the other woman's bed she drew back in horror.

There lay the other wife, whom she knew so well, with whom she shared every task of daily life, and yet how different she was. Everything about her seemed the same except for the horrifying fact that she had no head at all. Her body ended at the neck, and it was just as if a giant knife had sliced her in two like a piece of bread and carried her head away.

"It is the chonchon," whispered the second wife, realizing she was alone in the house with the two small children. "May the gods protect us all from the chonchon."

For she knew that the only explanation for this extraordinary event was that the first wife was a kalku, or witch, and at night, when every one is sleeping, the kalku has the magic power of detaching its head from its body and roving through the darkened world looking for adventure. When it does this it is called a chonchon. The kalku's ears become unusually large and strong, and flap like wings, so that the kalku can fly wherever it pleases. The cry of the chonchon when it flies is sad and mournful, and the Indians believe it is unlucky to be out at night and hear the melancholy cry, "Tué, tué, tué."

Ordinary people cannot see a chonchon, although they hear it; only other witches can actually see it.

The bravest people could try to drive it away by reciting a prayer backward, or drawing magic patterns on the ground. If this is done properly the chonchon will tumble down, unable to fly through the air, and remain helpless and unable to escape unless another chonchon happens to come by and rescue it.

But usually the very sound of "tué, tué, tué" makes people run for their lives, and lock themselves hurriedly inside their homes, and very few stay to drive the chonchon away.

So you can well imagine that this poor wife trembled with fright as she realized that there was actually a chonchon living with her in the same house. She stayed awake until her husband came home.

He was tired and drunk and ready to lose his temper.

"Why are you crying? Why are you awake? Why is the child crying? What has happened?" he demanded crossly.

"Go over to the other bed," said the wife, between sobs. "Go and see for yourself what has happened."

The husband stumbled across the room and was very surprised at what he found. He became angrier than ever, for no husband wants to feel that he is married to a witch, and, besides, he did not know how long this had been going on.

"Take both children with you and spend the rest of the night with friends," he told the second wife. "I will stay here and keep watch. Do not return until I send for you."

The poor woman was only too glad to do what he suggested, for she was trembling with fear, and it was impossible to sleep while she waited for the chonchon to come back. The two children were surprised to be dressed in the middle of the night, and kept asking to know the reason, but she told them they were going on a little visit and promised them a surprise the next day.

When his family had gone the husband very carefully turned the body of his chonchon wife over on its stomach, for all Indians know that the chonchon can only return to its earthly body when it is lying on its back.

Then he piled wood on the fire and settled himself beside it, ready to keep watch for the rest of the night.

Nothing happened until the first grey streaks of dawn tipped the sky. Then he heard an unusual sound at the door. It was like the wings of a giant bird brushing against it.

The Indian sat very still. He hardly dared to breathe. In the utter silence the beating sound could be heard louder still. Again the husband did not answer the call and open the door. Instead he piled more wood upon the fire, until it blazed so that its heat filled the room and the chonchon, waiting impatiently outside, could feel the warmth through the door. It began to beat more and more furiously upon the door, until the noise was deafening.

The Indian's heart pounded. "Who knows what the powers of the chonchon are?" he said to himself. "Yet in her human shape she is still my wife and the mother of my child. Perhaps I should let her return in case she becomes angry and harms us all."

He threw a pitcher of water over the fire, which hissed and crackled as it died down. Then he sat in a corner of the room and waited to see what would happen.

Suddenly the door burst open, and in the gathering light of dawn he saw a huge, clumsy bird fly into the room. It alighted on the bed of the absent wife, and when it saw that the body was turned over on its stomach it uttered such a despairing cry that the Indian's blood ran cold. Next it turned itself into a little dog, and ran over to the dead wet ashes of the fire, seeking some warmth. Then it went to the Indian, and with pathetic cries and movements of its body made signs begging the Indian to turn the body over again.

In spite of his earlier decision, the husband could not help feeling sorry for the unhappy creature, and he did what was wished. At once his wife gave a loud cry and sat up in bed, looking exactly the same as usual except that her face was badly scratched, as if she had been running through a grove of thorn-trees.

Her husband looked at her very sadly.

"Are you indeed a kalku?" he asked. "And have you been doing this night after night, while I knew nothing about it?"

His wife tried to calm his fears.

"Do not be afraid of me," she said. "I intend no harm to you nor to our family, but now that you know the truth there is no use in pretending any more. Every night, without your knowledge, I have gone out and travelled far and wide."

The Indian buried his face in his hands. He felt that he would never be able to live at peace with his wife again.

"Promise me," said the chonchon, "that you will not tell the village about what has happened, and in my turn I promise that no harm will ever come to this house."

He promised willingly, and next day when the other wife came back he made her promise too. The children were too small to understand what it was all about, and so the chonchon's secret remained well kept.

No harm ever came to that family, and the Indian never told this strange story until long after the chonchon herself was dead. By that time most of the villagers who knew her were dead too, and so it became just another tale that people told and remembered on dark stormy nights when you might expect to hear the eerie call of "tué, tué, tué" echoing across the fields.

How Nanco won a Wife

In a certain village there lived a man with a very pretty daughter. Although he was the cacique, the head man in the village, he was quite poor, for not long before his goods had been stolen by thieves, and now he did not even have an ox to help him on the land. The girl was so pretty that many men wanted to marry her, and her father thought it best to choose the richest of them all to be her husband. The girl protested, for this man was old and ugly, and blind in one eye besides.

"What does his eye matter?" asked the cacique crossly. "He is rich, and you will do well to marry him."

Now the girl secretly loved her cousin, Nanco, who was young and handsome, but as poor as the old man was rich. They both knew that her father would never consent to their marriage unless Nanco became rich.

One day the girl went to the lake to draw water as usual, and did not return to the house. Hours passed, but she was still absent. The cacique went out searching the countryside for her, and so did the rich old man with one eye, but they found no sign of her.

Among themselves the villagers argued about her disappearance, and in the end they all decided upon one thing.

"She must have been stolen by a sorcerer, a kalku," they agreed.

Nanco however was not dismayed. He was convinced that one day he would find her.

"One day I shall meet her and rescue her," he told the cacique firmly. "Then you will have to let us marry, and afterwards I shall make my fortune so that you will not be poor any more."

The cacique could no longer hope that the rich old man would wait for a bride who might never return, so he gave his nephew his blessing, and Nanco went off. First he journeyed to the forest, where he cut a bundle of twigs of the quisco, a thorny shrub. Then he went to the lake where the cacique's daughter had last been seen.

He saw floating upon the surface what appeared to be the skin of some animal, big and brown like a cow. The edges were full of countless eyes, and four extra large ones were set in the front of the creature. The Indians called this fantastic creature a *cuero*. Grasping his quisco twigs in his right hand, Nanco dived into the lake, and was ready to swim towards the *cuero* when it uprose like a great fish eager to swallow him.

But Nanco was ready. He held the twigs of quisco and hit at the *cuero* with them. Pricked by the thorns, the *cuero* collapsed like a balloon and flopped back on the water, beginning to sink.

When he saw what was happening Nanco jumped on top of the *cuero*, sitting on it like a raft. The *cuero* began to bleed from its wounds, and soon the lake waters were tinged with pink. At last it floated up against a huge tree-trunk which was half submerged in the lake. Nanco noticed that the tree formed part of the entrance to a cave right under the lake.

Slipping quietly as a fish, he swam into this cave. It seemed very dark until his eyes grew accustomed to the greeny-grey shadows. Then he saw a strange figure in front of him, a creature shaped like a man but with a head placed back to front, and his whole body round and fat like a bouncy ball. This creature did not see Nanco, for its head was turned the other way.

The young man braced himself for a tremendous leap forward. He seized the strange monster by the shoulders and twisted its head round. As it fell to the ground he plunged his knife into its stomach. There was a sharp hiss, a whistling sound, and air escaped from the monster, until it became a small shrunken thing which quickly died.

Nanco stood still a moment, listening intently, for he thought he heard voices coming from the back of the cave. Cautiously he moved forward, wondering what he would find. To his relief, there was nothing more frightening than several girls chained to the wall, and among them was his own sweetheart.

"Nanco, is it you?" she called, hardly able to believe she was saved.

He ran to her side.

"Tell me what happened, and how did the rest of you come to this cave?"

All talking at once, the girls explained that the *cuero* had captured each one as she came to the lake to draw water. It had dived deep down, dragging the girl with it, until they reached the cave. Here the other strange monster had been waiting. Some of the girls had been killed at once, the others were kept chained to the wall.

It was almost too much to realize that they were safe now, with nothing more to fear. Nanco promised that each girl should be on her way home that very day.

When he gave a last look round the cave he noticed that the stones which formed its walls were smooth and shone like metal, and smaller pebbles of the same rock littered the floor. He said nothing, but when he was unobserved picked up a fistful of the gleaming stones and hid them in the tree-trunk at the entrance to the cave.

"You will have to wait until I return with help," he told the girls, "but I shall be as quick as I can; and remember, you are quite safe now. Both monsters are dead."

He climbed on to the *cuero* raft and paddled with his hands until he reached the lake shore. Quickly he ran to the village and entered the cacique's house.

"Come at once," he cried breathlessly, "for I have found your daughter and all the other girls who have been lost these past years."

As word went round the village about Nanco's adventure every one came out to listen to him. They followed him to the lake, and chose a boat big enough to hold all the girls from the cave. Nanco dived down to lead them up, and soon each one was safely aboard. Then he dived down for the last time, and collected the stones which he had hidden in the tree-trunk.

Now that Nanco had rescued the cacique's daughter he thought that they would be able to get married at once, but his uncle pretended to be shocked at the idea.

"I gave my word she should marry my old friend," he objected. "I shall not break my word if he still wishes the wedding to take place."

Fiercely angry because he felt he was being cheated of something he had justly earned, Nanco hurried to the house of the rich old man.

"Do you still want to marry the cacique's daughter?" he demanded.

"Of course I do," replied the other.

"Then be ready to fight for her," shouted Nanco.

The two men fought long and hard on a deserted piece of ground away from every one. Nanco was younger and stronger, and in the end he won. The other man was wounded in his good eye, so that at the finish he was completely blind.

"I've had enough," he gasped; "you can take the girl!"

So the fight was over and the cacique agreed to let Nanco marry his daughter. Nanco took his pebbles, which were indeed valuable silver nuggets, to market, using some of them to buy a pair of oxen for his father-in-law, some lovely wedding clothes for his bride, and a fine horse with a splendid silver bridle for himself. Every one for miles around came to the wedding, and when his uncle died, some years later, Nanco became cacique in his place.

The Machi and the Nguruvilu

THERE WAS once in a certain part of Chile a deep river dividing two very fertile pieces of land. Many people lived on both sides of the river, and, of course, there were times when they wished to cross it and visit each other. The safest way was to use a boat, and many Indians had their own dug-out canoes, called wampus. Sometimes they crossed on a raft. But there were some people who wanted to cross by wading the ford. However, this became so dangerous that nearly every one who tried to cross at that place was drowned, although from either bank it looked perfectly safe.

The Indians on both sides agreed that it would be a good thing if the ford could be made safe.

"I have heard a machi say that the deaths are caused by an animal living in the river by the ford," said one of them.

"Do you know where this machi lives?" the others asked.

"Oh, yes; I can take you to him any time you like."

A machi is a good sorcerer, who has learned magic skills and developed powers to cure illness, drive away wicked spirits, and generally perform very useful deeds. A machi often trains himself for years to do these very special things, and so he is not expected to work for his living like ordinary people. You pay a machi as you would pay a doctor. You should always show machis very great respect, and it is said to bring good luck if you go out of your way to give them food and small gifts.

Now, this particular machi had believed for some time that a river monster of some kind was the cause of so many Indians being drowned at this ford. He was quite sure that his magical powers were strong enough to destroy this animal, but he was certainly not going to do it unless some one came along and offered to pay him for this difficult service.

So when the Indians came to the machi, bringing presents of two stately horses, complete with silver-wrought stirrups and bridle, he listened with sympathy and understanding to what they said.

"First of all," they began, "will you tell us if it is true that you have said our people drown in the ford because of an animal which lives there?"

"Yes, indeed," answered the machi, "that is perfectly true."

"And can you promise us that you can stop these deaths?"

The machi pretended to be quite offended at the very idea that anyone could suppose he was not capable of such a simple thing.

So the presents were ceremoniously handed over and accepted by the machi, and the very next day they all went to the river and stopped at the ford. The machi had brought many dried herbs with him, some of them plants which the Indians had never seen growing near their valleys. Each had its own special and magical use. Some the machi rubbed into his skin, others he swallowed, as a sure protection against the evil spirit who lived in the river.

Then he carefully took off all his clothes except the chirippa, which is a kind of skirt worn from the waist to the ankles and kept in place by a belt. The machi's belt was of heavily carved silver, and had been a present from a grateful village.

The Indians watched with bated breath while the machi waded into the river. At first the water did not come any higher than his knees. But as he walked slowly to the middle of the stream, he came suddenly to a part which was no longer shallow, but a very dangerous whirlpool.

Abruptly he dived into the whirlpool and was seen no more. A sigh of horror went up from the Indians on the bank. Only a few minutes passed, but to the watchers they seemed like hours. They could remem-

ber only too well the many friends and relatives who had been drowned at that dangerous ford. At last the machi reappeared, holding in his arms a strange little animal which at a distance resembled a dog.

This was not, however, a dog but the nguruvilu, what the Indians called a fox-snake.

"Here is the cause of your friends' deaths!" called the machi, holding the animal at arm's length for all to see.

Then he took out a bright silver knife which had been hooked into his belt. The sharp blade glinted in the sunlight.

"If *you* kill any more people," said the machi to the nguruvilu, "*I'll* kill *you*."

And as he said this he moved his knife slowly up and down in front of the animal's nose. Four times he repeated his threat, holding the nguruvilu tightly so that it could not escape, and bringing the knife uncomfortably close to the animal.

Then the machi continued, "I will cut off this little foot if you kill any more people," and again he moved the knife in front of the animal's foot.

"I will cut off these little ears if you kill any more people," said the machi, and he moved his knife in front of the animal's ears.

"I will cut off your tail," said the machi, "if you kill any more people," and he moved his knife up and down close to the animal's tail.

All this time the Indians were shouting and dancing and beating their drums. These were well known to be very important signs of magic, and not even the nguruvilu, who had caused so many deaths, could possibly resist the machi.

They watched him dive down into the whirlpool once more with the fox-snake still in his arms. They ceased their singing and dancing for the space of time that the machi was invisible, and it was suddenly so silent you could hear the water lapping against the river-banks.

As soon as the machi's head was seen breaking the surface of the water again the dancing, singing, and drumming broke out anew, louder, faster, and happier than ever. The Indians rejoiced that the machi was so clever.

"Your river will be safe for your people from now

onward," he told them. "No one else will ever be drowned here."

The Indians were very grateful and saw to it that the machi was given the best of everything at the feast that night, and next day he was escorted back to his home with more presents.

As for the river, nobody knows what happened to the nguruvilu, but it is indeed a fact that the whirlpool grew smaller and smaller, until by the end of the year it had disappeared entirely, and the ford itself became so shallow that a child could cross in perfect safety. And from that day to this, it is said, nobody has ever been drowned by crossing the river at that ford.

How the Poppies grew

IN THE SUMMER, when the corn is ripening, the dancing heads of red poppy flowers are a common sight, but it was not always so. Once there were no poppies at all, and this story tells how they grew overnight to lighten the sorrow of Rosaura's parents. Who was Rosaura? And why did her parents grieve?

Well, Rosaura was a mischievous little girl, who was loved and spoiled by all who knew her. She was always happy, and her laughter rang out like peals of bells in the courtyards and corridors of her father's home, so that the farm-workers called her Cascabelito, or Little Bell. Sometimes her mother and father wished that Rosaura did not always do just what she pleased, and instead was quiet and obedient like other little girls. But when she was with them they were charmed by her pretty, lively ways, and in the end gave way to her again.

Her mother often worried about her.

"Rosaura has no sense of danger," she would com-

plain fretfully. "Suppose one of the animals hurt her?"

But all the animals on the ranch knew and loved her, and Rosaura was fearless and trusted them all.

"Suppose one day she got lost?"

But Rosaura knew every lane, every corner of the ranch, like the back of her hand, and besides—every one there knew her, and there was always somebody near by to turn to if she needed help.

"Well, she ought to stop being a tomboy, and learn to behave like a proper girl. Why don't you speak to her about it?"

So Rosaura's father tried to scold her for wandering into the poultry-yard, so that her pretty frocks got dirty, and going into the corrals, where the cattle might knock her over, or climbing trees in case she fell down, or wandering too far away from the house into the cornfields.

"Rosaura! Rosaura! Where are you?"

Useless to expect the girl to return home of her own accord. Her mother would stand on tiptoe, looking for the telltale red handkerchief which was tied round the girl's rebellious curls, and which could be seen moving in the distance as Rosaura scampered away, deliberately refusing to listen to her mother's call.

"I'll go home in a minute," Rosaura would say to herself, "but just look at that lovely butterfly! I wonder if I can catch it!" And off she would go again, forgetting her mother in the enjoyment of the moment.

"Rosaura! *Rosaura*!"

Now there would be a commanding note in her mother's clear voice which the girl did not dare ignore. She knew that her mother must have seen her and was now determined to have her home. So Rosaura would start back, and from a distance her red handkerchief would look like a flower, sometimes seen and sometimes hidden, amid the golden ears of corn. As she approached the house she would dawdle, and her mother would start to scold her the moment she came in sight.

"In the cornfields again! In the sun again! How many times have I told you not to! When are you going to behave like other girls?"

Rosaura would hang her head while her mother's words fell like a shower of hail on the bushes, but it did not last, and an hour later Cascabelito's red silk handkerchief would once more be bobbing up and down as she ran all over the ranch.

She always came home in the end, although sometimes she was tired out and drowsy with too much sunshine. Then she would hide in a cool corner of the corridors of the house, hoping her mother would not see her and send her off to rest in bed.

One day she did not return at all for the midday siesta. At first her absence was not noticed. But when the day had grown cooler and the men were getting ready to leave the shade of the house in order to finish their work in the fields they became aware that it was all strangely silent. There was no sign of the child whose laughter and gaiety was so much a part of their lives.

"Where's Rosaura?" asked her father. "Has anyone seen Rosaura? Do you know where she is?"

But none of the men had seen her, and all began calling her name, and they searched high and low.

As time wore on it became clear that the little girl

had not returned, and every one grew worried. Never before had she stayed away from home during the midday siesta.

"Quick," ordered her father, "we must send out a search-party to the cornfields. The sun has been too strong for her. She must have collapsed and be lying ill somewhere."

"I've told her time and time again about being in the sun," Rosaura's mother exclaimed. "I've warned her that the sun can be dangerous, but she would never take any notice of me."

The farm-labourers hurried quickly to the cornfields, for they all loved the little girl and wanted to see her back safe and sound. But although they searched until the sun set and darkness was falling, there was no sign of her. Back they went to the house, tired and unhappy, but only to rest for a short time. Rosaura's father refused to believe that his daughter had disappeared for ever, and since he went on searching all through the night he made his farm-workers do the same.

He wandered all over the ranch, calling her name, and even if anybody had wanted to sleep that night those anxious cries for his missing Rosaura would have awakened them.

When the moon rose it shone on his unhappy figure, pushing a way through the shoulder-high sea of corn. The farm-workers accompanied him, but in the dark it was impossible to see anything. By dawn, utterly exhausted, they went one by one back to snatch a few hours' sleep.

Rosaura's mother, as grief-stricken as her husband, went out into the cornfields, and the unhappy parents searched and searched without rest. When the sun rose, and its first rays tinged the cornfields with glowing pink, they were too tired to speak to each other—and, after all, what was there to say?

Silently, hand in hand, they walked back along the path to the house. But every now and then, hoping against hope, they looked back at the corn, moving in the gentle morning breeze. Yet both of them were sadly aware Rosaura was gone for ever. Suddenly the father stopped. He could see something in the distance. Was it a trick of the eyes? Somewhere he was sure he had seen a scrap of red in the middle of the cornfield, like Rosaura's handkerchief.

"Look, look over there!" he exclaimed. "Don't you see something? A scrap of red?"

"Yes," said his wife. "But there's another one, and another, and another!"

"So there is! And again, there and there and there and there!"

To their astonishment, they saw that the whole cornfield was streaked with tiny red dots, reminding the parents so very much of the dancing red handkerchief of their little Rosaura. The father said in a disappointed way, "Flowers. Red flowers, that's all they are."

But the mother's eyes softened, and somehow she felt a little comforted. "How beautiful they are," she murmured, and her sorrow lessened.

Every one came to the cornfield, and as the day grew brighter they looked with wonder at these new, unknown red flowers, glowing and dancing in the corn. And this, so the Indians say, is how poppies were born. The witch who had stolen Rosaura away the day before had taken her red handkerchief, and transformed it into scarlet poppies, as a remembrance of the little girl to comfort those who had loved and lost her.

The Legend of Lake Aculeo

IN THE sixteenth century the Spanish conquistadores were storming through the Inca land of Peru, led by their commander Pizarro. As they conquered more and more territory some of their troops swept southward across the border into Chile. Pedro de Valdivia saw the fertile valleys of that country, and in 1541 he founded the city of Santiago.

It was not to be expected that the Chileans would accept the Spanish masters without fighting. For many years there were bitter skirmishes between the people of the old Chile who wanted to remain free and those who had joined the new rulers. Of all the Indian races in Chile the Araucanians of the southern forests were the proudest and most independent in their unyielding wars against the Spaniards.

But there were some people whose lives were already so pleasant, rich, and easy that they tried to keep away from the wars, to look after their own affairs, and to avoid joining in on either side. One of the happiest valleys was near Rancagua, which in those days was close to the agreed limit of Spanish territory. Beyond that point it was still the old Chile, with her customs and language.

Here in great style and peace of mind lived a community of wealthy Chilean farmers. Their estates were very large, their cattle sleek and healthy, their crops grew in abundance, and their houses were built to give both pleasure and shelter. So long as the Spaniards kept to their side of the border, these farmers did not trouble about the world beyond their own farms. They were friends with each other, visited their neighbors, and looked after their families and servants. They never worried about thoughts of the future.

One day, however, a messenger came with alarming news. It appeared that the Spaniards were no longer content just to build their beautiful city of Santiago, and some of their ambitious young captains had set their eyes on the lands beyond. At that very moment the area of Rancagua was being occupied by the Spanish invaders.

The oldest and richest of the farmers called his neighbors together so that they could discuss the best way of dealing with this new situation.

"Alas! we are simple farmers and not soldiers," lamented one of them. "Do you think we have any chance of fighting the Spaniards and of driving them back?"

"We can fight them, yes—but can we drive them back? Even the most warlike of our people have been defeated by them. The Spaniards come with horses and armour and weapons, the like of which we have never seen or needed. If they have made up their minds to invade this part of our beautiful land I'm afraid we cannot do much to stop them."

The younger men felt that this was too gloomy a view of things, but they were outnumbered by the older farmers, who thought of their wealth, and considered they had much to lose by fighting.

"It is well known that the Spaniards think of little else but precious treasure," said one. "And if they once realize that here in our quiet valley we possess the kind of gold and silver and precious stones that they most desire, their soldiers will ride through our fields, burning our houses and carrying away our treasure chests. Blood will be spilt and sorrow brought to our women and children."

Here the men looked at each other, nodding their agreement. It was perfectly true that on special occasions, like weddings and funerals, they ate and drank from vessels made of the finest silver, richly ornamented with gold and jewels. This was so much a part of their life that they took it for granted and thought no more of it than if they used cups and plates of thick red earthenware. To the covetous eyes of the Spaniards, however, things would look very different.

Although the farmers did not believe that gold and silver and precious stones were so important that a man should kill to gain possession of them, nevertheless they saw no reason why they should be tamely handed over to the invaders, and so they began to think of ways of safeguarding their wealth.

"If we could send our treasure across the high Andes and into the Argentine," said the richest of them, "that would save it. The Spaniards would not follow across those snowbound passes, nor do they know the country and the secret paths. Their horses would perish in the biting wind, and their soldiers would grow faint with mountain sickness. Besides, there is so much to keep the Spaniards here in Chile, and little to lure them over such a long and arduous trail."

"And who is to go with our treasure, may I ask?" said the greediest and most suspicious of all the farmers. "Do we all go so that each man may keep an eye on his own fortune?"

This led to more argument, and it looked as if there would be no end to the difficulties which one by one were raised by first one farmer and then another. Indeed, the hours sped by all too quickly, and still there was no agreement.

Finally, one of the young men pointed out that while they sat over their wine, arguing and coming to no decision, the Spaniards were undoubtedly gathering in strength in Rancagua, and could at any time make their appearance outside the farm gates.

This awareness of danger aroused them at last. Each farmer privately visualized only too clearly the horrifying sight of the tall, dark Spaniards—men of iron, clad in iron—mounted, confident, conquering. Then the wisest of the farmers, who was by no means the richest, spoke up.

"Our best plan," he suggested, "is for each of us to pack his goods in suitable boxes and bring them here to this farm as a collecting point. We will then put them in an ordinary, shabby ox-cart. The Spaniards, even if they passed it on the road, would never imagine that an ordinary cart, drawn by oxen, could possibly contain anything of value. Whereas if we put our wealth in our best and fastest carriage, the Spaniards would be sure to stop it and search it."

Every one felt this was an excellent idea, and they all agreed to it. But this was only the first step. There still remained the most important thing to be decided. Who was to be entrusted with the mission taking the most treasured possessions of all these wealthy farmers out of the country into the Argentine? Was there anyone among themselves who was sufficiently liked and trusted to be chosen as the man?

They could have argued about this all day without making up their minds. In the end they felt it would be safer if they chose some one who was not a farmer. After all, if the Spaniards recognized a prominent farmer driving an ox-cart along the dusty roads like some common servant, they would immediately wonder what was behind this unusual event. Apart from this, when it really came to the point, none of these rich men could be quite sure if in fact he could trust his neighbour.

But there was indeed one man—a poor servant on this very farm—older than all the farmers there, known and respected by all of them. His whole life had been spent in the service of his master, and his master's father before him, and of all the men in the whole valley there was no one more trusted by the rich farmers than he.

Accordingly this servant was called in to the room and informed of the plan. He listened carefully to every word.

"No matter what the cost," said his master solemnly, "the treasure entrusted to you must be saved from any possible danger. You may be called upon to make many sacrifices in guarding our fortune, so if you feel we are asking too much say so at once, and do not think we shall blame you for it. Nobody will think any the less of you."

But the servant would have been ashamed to refuse. He possessed no wealth, but his honor was dearer to him than life itself, and every one in the district knew it.

"I have spent all my life in your service," he said proudly. "Now, near the end of my days, I ask nothing better than to live out the rest of my life in your service. And if, indeed, it costs my life—well, death waits for all of us, and I am ready whenever I meet it."

"Very well," said his master, touched by his loyalty, "then swear by all the vows you hold most dear that no matter what may happen you will never allow our treasure to fall into the hands of the Spaniards."

The servant willingly swore this by everything he held most dear.

The treasure was brought in boxes that very night and loaded on a sturdy cart drawn by two oxen. Then, although he could barely see the way by the light of the thin sickle of a new moon, the loyal servant set off towards the distant crests of the lofty Andes.

Every now and then he applied the goad to his oxen to make them go faster. In this way he came at last to the shores of Lake Aculeo, which is not far from Santiago, the city which lay between him and the mountains. He knew that this would be a dangerous place, for the Spaniards had been settled at Santiago for some time, and it was only to be expected that he would meet some on the road.

Indeed, some distance away, he saw a group of armed Spaniards, who, catching sight of him at the same instant, spurred their horses towards him at a gallop.

The servant, whose eyes were keen in spite of his age, saw that there were several of them, and he debated with himself how best to avoid capture.

"If I throw my dagger at them," he murmured, "I may kill two or three of them, but what will I gain in the end? There are five or six of them, so the others would kill me and make off with the treasure. If that happens I have indeed failed in my mission to my masters. Nor is it seemly for a Chilean, even a poor servant like myself, to show cowardice and run away from the Spaniards. So my best plan is to hide."

Having reached this conclusion, he looked around for somewhere to hide, but, alas! there was no suitable place to be seen. The approach to the lake was flat, covered with short grass and low-growing flowers. There was not even a clump of trees to conceal the cart and oxen.

"Well, then," he said stoutly, with a shrug of his shoulders, "there is nothing left but the lake itself."

He gave a shrill cry to start the oxen up again, and applied the goad with all his strength, so that the startled animals plunged headlong, their hoofs sinking deeper and deeper as they drove forward into the soft, damp soil. The water rose above the axles of the wheels, but the loyal servant never hesitated, sending his obedient cattle farther and farther into the cold green depths of the lake. As the wheels sank into the spongy mud of the lake bed, the cart, heavy with its weight of gold and silver and precious gems, to say nothing of the driver, disappeared without trace, and the waters closed over it with scarcely a ripple to show what had happened.

From afar the troop of puzzled Spanish horsemen gazed in disappointed fashion towards the lake, unable to account for the disappearance of the driver and his ox-cart.

And from that day onward, so they say, if anyone comes near the shores of Lake Aculeo, and listens very, very carefully, they can hear the shrill cry of the loyal servant, driving his oxen onward. And the cry becomes fainter and fainter, until you would declare that its dying sounds come from the very depths of the lake itself.

Other titles from
THE HIPPOCRENE LIBRARY OF FOLKLORE . . .

Czech, Moravian and Slovak Fairy Tales
Parker Fillmore

Everyone loves a "Story that Never Ends". . . Such is aptly titled the very last story in this authentic collection of Czech, Moravian and Slovak fairy tales, that will charm readers young and old alike. Fifteen different classic, regional folk tales and 23 charming illustrations whisk the reader to places of romance, deception, royalty, and magic. "The Betrothal Gifts," "Grandfather's Eyes," and "The Golden Spinning-Wheel" are a few examples of the enchanting stories that make this collection of fairy tales a beautiful addition to any library.

Ages 12 and up
243 pages • 23 b/w illustrations • 5 1/2 x 8 1/4 • 0-7818-0714-X • W •
$14.95 hc • (792)

Fairy Gold: A Book of Classic English Fairy Tales
Chosen by Ernest Rhys
Illustrated by Herbert Cole

"The Fairyland which you enter, through the golden door of this book, is pictured in tales and rhymes that have been told at one time or another to English children," begins this charming volume of favorite English fairy tales. Forty-nine imaginative black and white illustrations accompany thirty classic tales, including such beloved stories as "Jack and the Bean Stalk," "The Three Bears," and "Chicken Licken" (Chicken Little to American audiences).

Ages 12 and up
236 pages 5 1/2 x 8 1/4 • 49 b/w illustrations • 0-7818-0700-X • W •
$14.95hc • (790)

Folk Tales from Bohemia
Adolf Wenig
This folk tale collection is one of a kind, focusing uniquely on humankind's struggle with evil in the world. Delicately ornate red and black text and illustrations set the mood. "How the Devil Contended with Man," "The Devil's Gifts," and "How an Old Woman Cheated the Devil" are just 2 of 9 suspenseful folk tales which interweave good and evil, magic and reality, struggle and conquest.
Ages 9 and up
98 pages • red and black illustrations • 5 1/2 x 8 1/4 • 0-7818-0718-2 • W • $14.95hc • (786)

Folk Tales from Russia
by Donald A. Mackenzie
From Hippocrene's classic folklore series comes this collection of short stories of myth, fable, and adventure—all infused with the rich and varied cultural identity of Russia. With nearly 200 pages and 8 full-page black-and-white illustrations, the reader will be charmed by these legendary folk tales that symbolically weave magical fantasy with the historic events of Russia's past.
Ages 12 and up
192 pages • 8 b/w illustrations • 5 1/2 x 8 1/4 • 0-7818-0696-8 • W • $12.50hc • (788)

Folk Tales from Simla
Alice Elizabeth Dracott
From Simla, once the summer capital of India under British rule, comes a charming collection of Himalayan folk lore, known for its beauty, wit, and mysticism. These 56 stories, fire-side tales of the hill-folk of Northern India, will surely enchant readers of all ages. Eight illustrations by the author complete this delightful volume.
Ages 12 and up
225 pages • 5 1/2 x 8 1/4 • 8 illustrations • 0-7818-0704-2 • W • $14.95hc • (794)

Glass Mountain: Twenty-Eight Ancient Polish Folk Tales and Fables
W.S. Kuniczak
Illustrated by Pat Bargielski
As a child in a far-away misty corner of Volhynia, W.S. Kuniczak was carried away to an extraordinary world of magic and illusion by the folk tales of his Polish nurse. "To this day I merely need to close my eyes to see . . . an imaginary picture show and chart the marvelous geography of the fantastic," he writes in his introduction.
171 pages • 6 x 9 • 8 illustrations • 0-7818-0552-X • W • $16.95hc • (645)

The Little Mermaid and Other Tales
Hans Christian Andersen
Here is a near replica of the first American edition of 27 classic fairy tales from the masterful Hans Christian Andersen. Children and adults alike will enjoy timeless favorites including "The Little Mermaid," "The Emperor's New Clothes," "The Little Matchgirl," and "The Ugly Duckling." These stories, and many more, whisk the reader to magical lands, fantastic voyages, romantic encounters, and suspenseful adventures. Beautiful black-and-white sketches enhance these fairy tales and bring them to life.
Ages 9 and up
508 pages • color, b/w illustrations • 6 x 9 • 0-7818-0720-4 • W • $19.95hc • (791)

Old Polish Legends
Retold by F.C. Anstruther
Wood engravings by J. Sekalski
Now available in a new gift edition! This fine collection of eleven fairy tales, with an introduction by Zymunt Nowakowski, was first published in Scotland during World War II, when the long night of the German occupation was at its darkest. The tales, however, "recall the ancient beautiful times, to laugh and to weep . . ."
66 pages • 7 1/4 x 9 • 11 woodcut engravings • 0-78180521-X • W • $11.95hc • (653)

Pakistani Folk Tales: Toontoony Pie and Other Stories
Ashraf Siddiqui and Marilyn Lerch
Illustrated by Jan Fairservis
In this collection of 22 folk tales set in Pakistan, are found not only the familiar figures of folklore—kings and beautiful princesses—but the magic of the Far East, cunning jackals, and wise holy men. Thirty-eight charming illustrations by Jan Fairservis complete this enchanting collection.
Ages 7 and up
158 pages • 6 x 9 • 38 illustrations • 0-7818-0703-4 • W • $12.50hc • (784)

Polish Fables: Bilingual Edition
Ignacy Krasicki
Translated by Gerard T. Kapolka
Ignacy Krasicki (1735-1801) was hailed as "The Prince of Poets" by his contemporaries. With great artistry the author used contemporary events and human relations to show a course to guide human conduct. For over two centuries, Krasicki's fables have entertained and instructed his delighted readers. This bilingual gift edition contains the original Polish text with side-by side English translation. Twenty illustrations by Barbara Swidzinska , a well known Polish artist, add to the volume's charm.
105 pages • 6 x 9 • 20 illustrations • 0-7818-0548-1 • W • $19.95hc • (646)

Swedish Fairy Tales
Translated by H. L. Braekstad A unique blending of enchantment, adventure, comedy, and romance make this collection of Swedish fairy tales a must-have for any library. With 18 different, classic Swedish fairy tales and 21 beautiful black-and-white illustrations, this is an ideal gift for children and adults alike.
Ages 9 and up
190 pages • 21 b/w illustrations • 5 1/2 x 8 1/4 • 0-7818-0717-4 • W • $12.50hc • (787)

Tales of Languedoc from the South of France
Samuel Jacques Brun
For children to older adults (and everyone in between), here is a masterful collection of folktales from the South of France. Thirty-three beautiful black-and-white illustrations throughout bring magic, life, and spirit to such classic French folk tales as "My Grandfather's Tour of France," "A Blind Man's Story," and "The Marriage of Monsieur Arcanvel." Travel to ancient castles, villages, and countrysides, and experience the romance and adventure in these nine stories.
Ages 12 and up
248 pages • 33 b/w sketches • 5 1/2 x 8 1/4 • 0-7818-0715-8 • W • $14.95hc • (793)

Twenty Scottish Tales and Legends
Edited by Cyril Swinson
Illustrated by Allan Stewart
Twenty enchanting myths take the reader to an extraordinary world of magic harps, angry giants, mysterious spells and gallant Knights. Amusingly divided into sections such as Tales of Battle and Pursuit, Kings and Conquests, and Tales of Daring, this book brings to life the legendary Scottish mythology of ages past. Eight detailed illustrations by Allan Stewart bring the beauty of the Scottish countryside to the collection.
Ages 9 and up
215 pages • 5 1/2 x 8 1/4 • 8 b/w illustrations • 0-7818-0701-8 • W • $12.50hc • (789)